$\varepsilon\rho$

THE COST OF SILENCE

THE COST OF SILENCE

MARGARET YORKE

COMPASS PRESS
* OXFORD * MELBOURNE *

First published in the United Kingdom in 1977 by Hutchinson

Compass Press Large Print Book Series; an imprint of
ISIS Publishing Ltd, Great Britain, and Bolinda Press, Australia
Published in Large Print 2000 by ISIS Publishing Ltd,
7 Centremead, Osney Mead, Oxford OX2 0ES,
and Australian Large Print, Audio and Video Pty Ltd,
17 Mohr Street, Tullamarine, Victoria 3043
by arrangement with the Curtis Brown Group Ltd

British Library Cataloguing in Publication Data
Yorke, Margaret
  The cost of silence. – Large
  print ed.
  1. Detective and mystery
  stories
  2. Large type books
I. Title
823.9'14 [F]

Australian Cataloguing in Publication Data
Yorke, Margaret
  The cost of silence/
  Margaret Yorke
  1. Large print books
  2. Detective and mystery
  stories, English
I. Title.
823.914

ISBN 1–74030–128–5 (hb) 1–74030–129–3 (pb)
(Bolinda Publishing Pty Ltd)
ISBN 0–7531–6158–3 (hb) 0–7531–6265–2 (pb)
(ISIS Publishing Ltd)

Printed and bound by Antony Rowe, Chippenham and Reading

"As a rule, the game of life is worth playing . . ."

Dean Inge

CHAPTER
ONE

From the window above the shop Emma watched all that went on in the square. She saw the motorists going to work, and the school buses; the scooters and motor-bikes and the few cyclists. She saw retired men escaping from domestic imprisonment and housewives bound for the shops. At night, when the traffic on the main road slackened and she lay in bed reading a romance from the library, she would put down her book and listen; then she would hear an occasional car, the roar of a motor-cycle, the late bus from Muddington, and sometimes, in the distance, the barking of dogs out for a last run. The night sounds excited her, reminding her that there was another world beyond the restrictions of her own.

Norman watched the passers-by too, but it was the women he noticed. Mrs Hallam, smartly dressed, with two miniature dachshunds on long red leads, was always early. Later came Mrs Costello, with her wild white hair, shabby sheepskin coat and fat spaniel, relics all of better days spent in a small manor house amid seven acres. That was before her husband shot himself, leaving her little but debts. By the time young Mrs Armitage appeared with Simon in his pram on her way to Bodger's Self-Service the morning was nearly over.

Norman Widnes had run the ironmonger's shop since his father's sudden death from a heart attack; by then his mother's illness had begun. At first she helped him, and for a long time she kept the books, but gradually she was able to do less and less, until she took to sitting upstairs by the window watching what went on outside.

That was five years ago, before it all happened. Now there were just the two of them, and it was Emma who sat there, perpetually waiting.

Once again, Jamie Renshaw was late for school because the Alsatian that lived in Foster Avenue was waiting to gobble him up. Though he had turned back and gone all the way round by the square, he still wasn't safe, for a small white dog stood in the road opposite the ironmongers shop. He held his breath as he went past, and it ignored him.

Miss Baxter was cross when she found him sitting at his desk in the classroom after assembly.

"That's twice this week you've been late, Jamie," she said. "And it was three times last week."

"I'm sorry, Miss Baxter," Jamie mumbled, head bent, inspecting the scratches on top of his desk.

It was better to be in trouble at school than eaten alive by a wolf. Sometimes in the afternoons, his mother and baby sister met him, and they would all pass the Alsatian then; his mother always admired it, saying she would like one the same. Jamie lived in dread of this wish's fulfilment, but luckily his father said such big dogs needed a lot of exercise, and it wasn't fair to keep them in towns.

2

Across the square in Old Bidbury, facing the shops, Mrs Minter lived in a small Georgian house separated from its neighbours by a footpath which led over fields to the railway. Until recently, she had run an antique business in New Bidbury with a friend, but when the lease of the premises ran out the friend retired with her share of the capital, and now Mrs Minter was seeking a new interest for hers. Meanwhile, unused to having time to spare, she had taken to walking miles in the district, and as she walked she noticed everything. She often saw the Alsatian which alarmed Jamie Renshaw; it usually stood outside the home of its owner, Paula Curtis, a sculptor, and it barked at all who passed.

The house next door to Paula's was empty and had been up for sale for months; it was built in mock Tudor style, with false beams superimposed, and stood in a glade of straggly cupressus trees from among which protruded the agent's board. People saw over it and were dashed by the need to replumb and repair; they sighed over the tangled garden and did not come back. It was still for sale, Mrs Minter saw, on Thursday morning. As she went past the Alsatian barked at her, and from somewhere nearby came the sound of a child crying, but Mrs Minter was only dimly aware of it because the dog made much more noise.

"Jamie Renshaw was late for school again today," said Felicity Baxter that afternoon.

It was early closing day, when Norman went off in his van after shutting the shop to see to his business affairs, finishing his round at Felicity's flat which was on the top floor of an old house in a residential area of the town beyond the railway line.

Today he had arrived before she got home; he had brought some daffodils and arranged them in a jug. She had to admit that he was a very considerate lover, but now she disengaged his hands from round her waist, her mind still at school with the children. It had not always been like this: once she had been impatient and eager; but now she had to unwind first.

Norman, absorbed in his second life when he pretended that he lived with Felicity all the time, was willing to show interest in Jamie.

"I don't know him," he said. "At least, not by name — by sight, perhaps."

"He lives in Lincoln Close. His father used to bring him to school but he comes on his own now. It's not far, and he's old enough, but I wonder —"

She had moved away from him while she talked and was now in her bedroom, her voice coming to him through the open door. He caught glimpses of her as she passed back and forth putting her coat in the cupboard, and sitting on the end of her bed to take off her boots. He half rose, tempted to go in after her, but she reappeared before he could do more than start the action and he sank back. Things could be better if you waited for them, a reflection with which he often consoled himself as he stood in Emma's room listening to her heavy breathing in the night.

Felicity was still talking about Jamie.

4

"There's a new baby," she said, "He may be a bit jealous, you know, after being the only one for so long. But she must be a year old by now, if not more."

"Perhaps his mother's just late sending him off," Norman suggested. "Now that she's busier."

"Trust you to think of the simple solution," said Felicity, coming back into the room. "You could be right."

She smiled at him. She was feeling better now; the slight headache she'd had all day had lifted.

Norman forgot about Jamie Renshaw and kissed her. They were almost the same height.

"You," she said, suddenly filled with affection for him.

Norman wrapped his arms round her sturdy body in its Shetland sweater, crushed her to him so that he could feel the softness of her breasts against his chest, and said, "Don't ever leave me, Felicity. I don't think I could bear it if you did."

Felicity, responding to him, postponed, not for the first time, the moment when she told him that this was exactly what she intended to do.

Mrs Minter had guessed about Norman and Felicity. She had often seen him walk past her house down the footpath to the fields and the railway line; she walked that way herself when the weather was good. Once she had seen him cross the cutting and enter one of the large old houses that backed on to it. Most of these houses had been turned into flats, and on another occasion she had seen Felicity drive up to the same house in her red Fiat.

He could, of course, be visiting someone else, but Mrs Minter felt sure it was Felicity, whom she had met at an open day at the school. Because of her new-found leisure she had become more involved in local life and had enlarged her acquaintance. Like most people in Old Bidbury, she had been surprised when Norman married Emma almost immediately after his mother's death. Within a year, Emma had had a stroke which had left her partly paralysed. She spent all day on a sofa propped up so that she could look out of the window. With her good arm she could switch on the electric kettle which was kept on an asbestos pad on the floor beside her, operate the radio and the television, and she even managed a little simple embroidery in very large stitches. She could hobble about with a walking aid, and had an immense appetite for food, so that by now she was gross, eyes sunk in folds of flesh, her once red hair streaked with white. Over four years had passed since this had happened, and two years ago Norman had begun to look just a little less defeated; that was when it had started with Miss Baxter, Mrs Minter thought. But with no hope for the future, wouldn't the girl tire of it, eventually?

CHAPTER
TWO

On Friday morning Norman was stocking the till with the day's float when there was a squeal of tyres outside.

Through the glass door of the shop he could see a white mongrel terrier standing in the road, and a small boy, looking petrified, on the kerb at the far side. A Ford Cortina had stopped, and as Norman watched the driver got out and began scolding the child.

Norman slid the catch up on the door of the shop and went over.

"What's up?" he said, interrupting the flow of words pouring from the driver.

"Little wretch stepped off the kerb right in front of me — I had to swerve to avoid a dog — I might have killed him," raged the man. "Is he your kid?"

"No. On your way to school, are you?" Norman asked the boy.

"Yes," said Jamie Renshaw, ashen-faced.

"Your car'll block the traffic, left there," Norman pointed out to the driver.

Muttering, the man went back to it, and Norman turned to the child.

"Are you Jamie Renshaw?" he asked.

"Yes," said Jamie, showing no surprise at Norman's omniscience.

"This isn't your best way to school, is it?"

"No. But I can't go along Foster Avenue because of the wolf," said Jamie.

Norman understood at once.

"Mrs Curtis's Alsatian," he said. "You'll be late."

"I know, but I have to go the long way round," said Jamie.

"No, you don't," said Norman, making a quick decision. "I'll go with you." It wouldn't take long.

They strode off together, small, slight man and very small boy, back the way Jamie had come along Funnel Lane, into Lincoln Road and round to Foster Avenue.

The Alsatian was there, sniffing round a lamp-post, and he barked at them, but Norman knew it was habit and not hostility. He took Jamie's hand and they marched past. The dog approached, sniffed at them, then lost interest.

"He should be kept in," said Norman, aware that his companion was trembling. "But he won't hurt you."

Jamie was not convinced, but a hundred yards on his courage returned.

"Thanks very much, Mr Widnes," he said, and sped off up the road to the school.

Well, one small mystery was now solved, Norman reflected: the reason for Jamie's unpunctuality had been discovered. He would be able to tell Felicity about it.

"That mongrel will cause an accident one day," Emma said, when he returned. She had seen the incident from the window and knew that the white dog was let out

8

daily when its owners left for work and abandoned until their return at night.

"There's no law about keeping dogs under control, more's the pity," said Norman. "That Alsatian should be kept in too."

"Rub my back, Norm, before you go down, there's a love," Emma asked him, so he rolled her over, took out the talcum and for nearly five minutes gently massaged the huge rolls of flesh over her spine. She did not get dressed until Mrs Bowling arrived to help her.

When Norman went down to the shop again, his assistant, Madge Pearce, was weighing out nails for the Alsatian's owner, Mrs Curtis. Madge had replaced a youth who had left the shop because he never stayed anywhere longer than three months. Norman had been doubtful about employing her for she had only just left school, but he had never had a more willing helper. She was a stout girl with persistent acne, and, plain herself, was not repelled by Emma. If things were quiet in the shop she would go up and chat to her. She had once even washed her hair when Mrs Bowling, who usually did it, was away with flu.

Mrs Curtis's dogs, outside in the station wagon, were barking in chorus while Madge carefully tipped out nails into the scoop on the scales. She owned four besides the Alsatian.

"Good morning, Mrs Curtis," said Norman.

"Morning," said Paula Curtis. "Got to fix a broken fence."

"Oh," said Norman. "Is it a big job?" Perhaps this explained the Alsatian's freedom.

"No — won't take long," said Paula, and went off, a squat figure in grubby corduroy trousers, a duffle jacket and rubber boots. Norman saw her toss the parcel into the back of the wagon among the dogs. A small child with a white face and dark, untidy hair peered out of the side window. She sat on the rear seat, with the Alsatian perched beside her. The other dogs were behind, their heads leaning over her. Norman imagined their breath, strong-smelling, and the long, rasping tongues.

"I shouldn't like to be sat there, among them dogs," said Madge, expressing just what Norman was thinking.

"She doesn't seem to mind," he said. "The kid I mean."

"Used to it, I suppose," Madge remarked. She loved Norman dearly. He never teased her, wouldn't let her carry the heavier goods although she was just as strong as he was, and was always so polite even when telling her what to do. Madge's life had been transformed from the day she entered his employment for she knew she was needed. Who wanted to hang about giggling at the bus stop, waiting to be noticed by some spotty boy, when their days were spent with Mr Widnes? Madge occupied her evenings in washing her hair and putting anti-pimple cream on her face, or reading the magazines passed on to her by Emma.

As Norman watched Madge hurry forward to attend to a new customer, he was thinking that the weekend was coming, and with it Emma's birthday. He would not be able to see Felicity on Saturday night, as he usually did, when Emma thought he was at The Grapes.

Felicity was cutting up fragments of cloth for the children to make into collages. Everyone enjoyed this activity and while the children worked busily at their designs, Felicity was able to let her mind stray from the task in hand.

What a coward she had been, the day before. Once again, when her mind was made up to tell Norman that it must end between them, he had disarmed her. It was unfair of him to make capital of his dependence on her; everyone knew that his domestic life was a strain, tied as he was to an invalid wife much older than himself. People said Emma could not live for long; but how long was long? It might be years. Any permanent future for Felicity with Norman could be only a remote dream, and she was not even sure if it was something she wanted. Meanwhile, her involvement with him was denying her other opportunities — not that there were many in Bidbury. That was, perhaps, why she had slipped into this in the first place. They had met, in the most banal way, when she went into the shop to buy a hand-drill and fitments to put up some shelves. He had told her the best place to buy timber, and after that, whenever she went into the shop, they would discuss what other improvements she planned. Then, one Thursday afternoon when it was raining, he had passed her in his van. She was walking back from school because her car was in dock. Norman had given her a lift; she had asked him in, and so it had begun.

She soon found that the impression of diffidence he gave was misleading; as a lover he was assured and tender. She had invited him into her flat the day their affair began because she was bored and lonely, but she wanted more from life than this limited relationship. Next Thursday she would stick to her resolve and tell him so.

"Perhaps Mrs Curtis will mend her fence over the weekend and keep that dog in," said Emma, when Norman told her about Paula Curtis buying the nails.

"Maybe he'll be at home for once and do it for her," said Norman.

"I'm sure she's well able to do it herself," said Emma. "She's very capable. She's got to be. He's not like you."

She stretched out a podgy hand to Norman, the fingers like sausages. She wanted him to caress her. Before she could utter the direct invitation, Norman got up and switched on the television.

"You watch *Nationwide* while I get supper," he said.

He went out of the room, across the landing to the kitchen, and Emma, propped on the large sofa, gazed after him sadly, not deceived.

Automatically, she popped a chocolate cream into her mouth. Dr Barrett scolded her, every time he came, for eating such a lot; she'd dig her grave with her teeth, he said. But what else was there for her to enjoy?

In the kitchen, Norman was filled with shame. A kiss was little enough to give. He would make amends later, he resolved, neatly dicing cold chicken so that Emma could eat it with a fork. He gave great thought to their meals, refusing Emma the steamed puddings and the pastries that she loved. Mrs Bowling, who cleaned the flat and cooked their midday meal every day, brought in sweets and biscuits on the sly and hid them among Emma's possessions. Norman knew it, but he had not the heart to prevent it. He salved his conscience by providing salad and fruit and lean meat, and was, himself, extremely thin.

Sometimes, usually at three in the morning when he could not sleep, Norman would acknowledge that if Emma grew still heavier and threw more strain on her heart, it would all come to an end; if he really wanted to avoid this he would confiscate the hidden titbits and forbid Mrs Bowling to provide more. Perhaps, though, he needed Emma as much as she needed him; at his lowest ebb he would remember how it all began, when his mother was so ill and Emma had suddenly arrived, full of an irresistible warmth. There had been magic then.

It didn't do to look back too far. Some things were best forgotten: those blue capsules, for instance, emptied into that final drink.

Norman took Emma her tray. Then he bent and kissed her cheek, feeling the soft texture of her skin against his lips.

"There, dear. Doesn't that look tasty?"

He laid his own place at the table, where later he would do the books. They kept the television on, so there was no need for conversation.

CHAPTER
THREE

Madge loved Saturday. It was the busiest day of the week in the shop and she was on the go the whole time. Mr Widnes could never manage without her, she was happily certain.

This Saturday she had brought Emma an African violet for her birthday. Emma was delighted with it, and it was on the window-sill beside her when Madge went up at half-past ten for tea.

The electric kettle stood on the floor and Emma had switched it on, but her arms were so flabby that pouring the water was difficult for her. Madge made the tea and while it stood she fetched Emma a chocolate biscuit from the tin they secretly kept in Emma's capacious sewing-bag. She was making a tapestry cushion in large, simple stitches; Mrs Bowling, who would be arriving soon, had sent for the wool and canvas from a magazine.

"Norman will catch us one day," said Emma, crumbs sticking to her chin.

Madge ate a biscuit too, just as guiltily, for she knew it was bad for her spots.

"Never mind," she said. "He wouldn't be really cross."

"Don't you believe it," said Emma. "You don't know him like I do."

For her lunch Madge brought sandwiches and ate them in the store-room while the shop was closed, or on fine days in the small garden where Norman grew vegetables. Up in the flat Norman, Emma and Mrs Bowling would consume mince, liver, steamed fish, or other such non-fattening fare. Mrs Bowling came every day except Sunday and stayed until three. On Thursdays, early closing day, she stayed until ten-thirty so that Norman could have the proper break which Emma insisted he needed. Mrs Bowling and Emma spent these evenings playing cards.

Before he met Felicity, Norman went to the cinema on Thursdays; now he still pretended that he did so, reading up about what films were showing in New Bidbury and in Muddington in the local paper. At first, lying about them to Emma was difficult, but now it was quite easy and in any case she never showed much curiosity.

Norman and Madge, between them, kept the shop clean. Madge lived across the railway and came to work on the bus. Her father was an electrical fitter who travelled about mending and servicing washing machines and vacuum cleaners, her mother worked in the dry-cleaners in New Bidbury, and her brother Reg at a local factory. Madge, the butt of teasing at home from Reg and from both boys and girls at school, loved the privacy of her lunch hour at work. She never thought about anything particular then unless it was the next task she would perform in the service of Mr Widnes, but she was aware, though she could not have defined it, of her own utter contentment.

This Saturday she missed her usual bus and so walked home down the path past Mrs Minters and over the railway. Her mother had said she should not go that way after dark, but Reg had mocked and said that no one was going to bother to do old Madge; whoever would want to?

"That's enough," their father had frowned. He was ashamed of his daughter's plainness but he felt an irritated affection for her.

"Ah — there you are, Madge," said her mother that evening. "You're late, dear."

Madge explained that she'd helped Mr Widnes cash up and empty the till. There was ever such a lot of money in it.

"What does he do with it over the weekend?" asked Reg, who was cleaning his boots before going out for the evening.

"That's his business," said Madge. Why should she tell Reg about the safe in the wardrobe upstairs?

"Stuffs it under his old woman, maybe," said Reg. "It'd be safe enough there. Whoever'd move her?"

Madge bristled angrily.

"Mrs Widnes is ever so nice, poor thing," she snapped.

"It's very sad, as we know," said their mother in a soothing voice. She hated their squabbles. "Now come on, you two. Sit down. Tea's ready."

"Where's Dad?" asked Madge.

"Out," said their mother flatly. "We won't be waiting."

She knew that he'd found a new woman; there were too many temptations on his kind of job.

"How'd he come to marry her? That Widnes?" Reg was asking between mouthfuls of sausage and chips. "Old enough to be his mum, isn't she?"

"No." Mrs Pearce could remember seeing Emma in the shop in those early days. "Much older than him, yes, but not that old. She was a good-looking woman."

Emma had been stout then, but handsome; she'd had thick red hair, bright eyes, and a way with her that made you like her at once. Harry, Mrs Pearce's husband had admired her a lot. It seemed that she and Norman's parents had met years before, on holiday, the story went. Emma, passing through Bidbury, had seen the name Widnes over the shop and called on impulse. When she saw how ill Norman's mother was, she'd moved in and taken the household in charge. She'd been recently widowed herself, it was said, so it answered a problem for her too.

Almost immediately, things changed. Norman stopped looking like a wraith himself; his mother grew more cheerful and was certainly more comfortable, until, after nearly a year, she died.

There had scarcely been time to wonder what Emma would do now before the wedding was a fact.

On Saturday evenings Emma encouraged Norman to go round to The Grapes. Nowadays, though, he spent only a short time at the pub and then went to Felicity's flat. However, because this Saturday was Emma's birthday, he had to stay at home. Jack Phelps, who ran the local garage, was coming with his wife to spend the evening.

Felicity went to the cinema with Elsie Dawes another teacher, and afterwards, in a pub, they discussed their plans for Easter. While they were talking some youths came into the bar, swaggered up to the counter and noisily ordered their drinks.

"They've seen too many television commercials about the manliness of drinking beer," said Felicity sourly.

"Hope they don't make a scene," said Elsie, who was comfortable where she was and wanted another rum and coke before she went home.

The youths were full of physical energy; even their hair, long and carefully styled, seemed to crackle with vitality. They postured and preened themselves like young cockerels.

"Easy enough to break a window," one said, and Felicity, startled, began to listen to them.

"Someone'd see. There's always folks about. Besides, it wouldn't be kept in the till," she heard.

One of the boys noticed her looking their way and nudged the speaker.

"Bit old for us, them birds," he said. "Been plucked, already."

Amid titters the youths began to discuss where they would go in search of more promising talent.

"Silly kids," said Elsie, but she spoke tolerantly.

Felicity found them frightening. They were not necessarily lawless, merely misdirected — the sort of young men who could prove heroic in an emergency, such as war. It sounded, now, as if they might be contemplating some sort of break-in. She wondered if the police ought to be warned. She was still wondering when Reg Pearce and his friends left the pub.

"They're taking Emma out," said Mrs Minter.

It was Sunday, and she was standing by the window pouring out sherry for Mrs Costello, who had come to lunch after going to church. Mrs Minter never went to church but Mrs Costello always did, partly from habit and partly because it helped to pass the time. She vaguely hoped, also, that in some after life there would be a chance for her to ask Charles why he had not told her about his financial troubles instead of killing himself and leaving her to face them eventually, but alone. Though it had happened ten years ago, she was still haunted by the memory of finding him in the field below the house, the gun he used for shooting rabbits by his side.

"Emma Widnes? Going out?" Mrs Costello said.

"Yes. I thought they'd given up taking her," said Mrs Minter.

Mrs Costello joined her at the window. Across the square a large old Rover was drawn up outside the ironmonger's, and Emma, supported on one side by Norman and by an older, burlier man on the other, was tottering through the wide entrance of the shop.

"However did they get her down the stairs?" wondered Mrs Minter.

"That's Jack Phelps, from the garage," said Mrs Costello. "They must be going for a drive."

"Well, Norman is marvellous," said Mrs Minter. "He seems to be devoted to her." Though what about his trips

19

across the fields to see the schoolmistress? She gave Mrs Costello her sherry. "Here you are, Jane. I'll just have a look at the joint."

They were having half a shoulder of lamb. She knew that Mrs Costello did not bother to cook properly for herself, and unless invited out was likely to start drinking and forget about food. In an exasperated way she was fond of the older woman, and felt obliged to keep an eye on her.

Mrs Costello and her spaniel lived in a small, old house wedged between Bodger's Self-Service and the greengrocer, two doors away from Widnes' Stores. Her garden was longer than Norman's and ran right down to Lincoln Road at the end, where there was a way out through a wicket gate. In summer she had the finest show of flowers in the district, the one factor she had brought to Bidbury from her former life. She worked in the garden constantly while Pedro rootled about beside her. Mostly, she and Pedro were companionably silent, but sometimes she would talk to him, and he only yapped in protest when he was left alone.

Now she stood at her friend's window and shamelessly watched while the great bulk of Emma Widnes was levered into the car. Norman got in beside her, and Jack Phelps, wiping a hand across his heated brow, clambered behind the steering wheel. As they drove off, Mrs Costello saw a white, moon-like face peering out of the side window.

She wondered where they were going, and how they would ever get Emma upstairs again.

Norman wondered the same thing. Emma had not been out of the flat since the summer. Jack Phelps, a kindly man, had suggested the outing as they celebrated her birthday the previous evening.

Well, here they were, driving off. They'd somehow got her down, a step at a time, and somehow they'd get her up again.

The pale sun, low in the wintry sky, shone as they left the square. Three youths who had been sprawling on the seat in the bus shelter saw them go.

"She does go out, then, of a Sunday," one remarked. "How long'll they be, I wonder?"

They all got up and slouched over the road to peer in at the window of Norman's shop. Oil heaters, rolls of wire, netting, garden tools and so forth were to be seen within, and several tiered columns of saucepans. The till was clearly visible on the counter at the rear.

Reg Pearce had only been showing off his knowledge when he aired the subject in the pub the night before. In theory it would be quite a laugh to see if they could grab the lot, but it was more the lark of trying it that appealed to him than getting the money. He had a good job, and plenty left in his pay packet after his mother had received her share.

He supposed it did no actual harm to look at the shop, however; it didn't mean they'd try anything.

Norman, beside Emma in the car, patted her soft white hand.

"Well, dear. All right, are you?"

Emma looked out at the scene beyond the warm box of the car, hiding a sigh. She had exchanged one prison

21

for another. They would drive to some country pub, bring her a drink to the car, and then drive home again. Jack Phelps had suggested the trip on impulse when the weather forecast was good. If all went well and she seemed to enjoy it, they'd do it again, and a further huge effort would be required from her.

"Lovely, dear," she said. She clasped Norman's hand and held it against her vast thigh. "You're good to me, Norm."

In the mirror Jack Phelps saw Norman look away from her out of the window, his face white and strained, his jaw set.

"Spring's coming," said Mr Phelps cheerfully. "There's lambs in the valley. We'll go that way, shall we?"

Emma's heart was thumping uncomfortably and she felt rather breathless. Still, they meant to be kind, taking her out like this; it would never have done to refuse. And it was nice having Norman beside her, close, like they used to be.

"Lovely, Jack," she gasped.

The boys could see no easy way into Norman's shop from the front. It was wedged between the newsagent's and the greengrocer's, and the shop door was the only entrance.

"Maybe there's a way in at the back," said Terry.

"Oh — let's leave it," said Reg. "What's the point?"

"Don't know till we try," said Mick Green.

They slouched off across the square and down Funnel Lane into Lincoln Road. Here, the gardens of the buildings on one side of the square ended in fences varying in solidity. They walked along, whistling. Mick Green, the biggest of the three, ran his hand along the palings; he picked up a splinter off one, and made a fuss about it. Reg, with large, grimy fingers, prised it out.

Behind Bodger's Self-Service there was a drive-in, and Bodger's van could be seen there; also, beside it, was Norman's small green van. His name was neatly painted on its side. If he kept it there, it must mean his shop had no back entrance, reasoned Mick.

Then they saw Mrs Costello's gate, a wicket one in her fence. Mick was through it in a flash, and making his way up the garden.

Suddenly a high, irate barking came from the house. Pedro, shut in while his mistress was out, was defending the property.

Mick dashed out again at speed, and the three boys ran up the road laughing.

"No good, you see," said Reg, very relieved.

"There's ways of making dogs quiet," said Mick.

"Bet you can't do it — get in and get the loot," said Terry.

"How much?" asked Mick.

CHAPTER
FOUR

"Our children must learn to relate to nature," said Lydia Renshaw in the voice she had used when she taught home economics before her marriage. "It's particularly important when they're growing up in an urban environment."

Geoffrey, intent on the *Sunday Express*, did not look up.

"Mm," he said.

"You're not listening," Lydia accused.

"I am — it's important that the children appreciate nature," he said, masking a sigh. Lydia's earnestness started operating the moment she awoke each morning.

"Relate to, not just appreciate," she said. "We ought to get a puppy. You'd like that, wouldn't you, Jamie?" she asked her son. "Perhaps it could be your very own." Luckily she did not wait for an answer but swept on. "Animals communicate on a different level from us. Learning to live with them is a special art. It deepens the meaning of life."

Jamie heard his mother in an agony of fear.

"There's Claire now, too," she pointed out. "The sooner we get a dog the better — they can all grow up together."

"Why?" asked Geoffrey. "It's different for people who are alone, like poor old Mrs Costello, who needs a dog for company, but we don't. We've got one another."

Jamie felt like cheering at these staunch words.

"I'm going to wash the car. Coming to give me a hand, Jamie?" asked Geoffrey, abandoning the paper.

Thankfully, Jamie followed him into the garden.

"I don't like dogs very much, Dad," he confided as they bent to sponge the bumper of the Vauxhall.

"What? Don't you?" To Jamie's dismay his father did not look pleased. "Not afraid of them, are you?"

"Oh no! No, of course not," Jamie said hastily.

He wasn't really: only of big, fierce ones, he told himself. But all dogs had a way of sniffing at you that he didn't really like.

"Because if you are, we must get one as your mother says," his father told him. "To get you over it. Can't have that sort of thing."

That Sunday night, Norman lay wakeful in bed, unable to stop his racing mind as it played back to him a film of the day. Somehow, after her outing, they had got Emma up the stairs, but she'd had to pause halfway for over ten minutes, getting her breath back, and when they reached the top she'd looked very blue. It hadn't been worth the effort; he knew that short of a miracle she would never come down again.

"You're very good to me, Norm," she'd repeated. "Fat useless old bag that I am."

"Don't talk like that," he'd answered, wanting to add that he owed her so much, but the words wouldn't come out.

25

Who owed whom what, he wondered now, staring up in the darkness at the ceiling, and when did payment cease? His door was propped ajar, so that if she called out in the night he would hear her. They'd lain in here together when his mother was dying, listening, the two of them, in the same sort of way. Only when she had sunk into a heavy, drugged sleep had they felt free from restraint. Norman was confident that she'd never suspected them.

Those had been wild months. Looking at Emma now, it was difficult to believe it had not been some fantasy. With Felicity he had a much calmer relationship, but under it, never mentioned, was a sense of futility. He was paying now for what happened years ago, binding him and Emma irrevocably together.

Emma was awake too. Her heart thumped and her breathing was difficult, but she had taken her pills and soon she would drowse off. It would take her days to get over this morning's expedition.

Norman was very patient. How would things have turned out for him if she had not arrived in his life when she did, Emma wondered. He'd been so ardent; Emma could still smile, remembering him then, but soon tears would come to her eyes to think that it was all over. She could sense his reluctance now whenever he so much as kissed her. Once, it had been so different.

Norman never left the sleeping tablets within her reach: her heart pills, yes, but not the barbiturates.

"I don't want an accident," he had said.

It had not been an accident four years ago, and what had happened before could happen again. He would come to it in the end, she was certain.

Paula Curtis cut up the dogs' meat on the drainer in the kitchen. She had a large knife in one big red hand; the other, holding the raw meat, was stained with blood. Around her in the kitchen were ranged her canine pack, in an expectant semi-circle. Excited whimpers came from the Alsatian and the collie. Her two bulldogs leaned forward on their stumpy front legs, panting. Only the Labrador which belonged to Guy, her husband, was absent.

"Well, my boys, hungry then, are you?" Mrs Curtis inquired of them, chopping away. "All in good time, my lovely lads."

She went on talking while she portioned the meat into five bowls. Somewhere among them rested a small cabbage, and a chicken divested of its polythene bag, semi-thawed. A half-full bottle of milk was nearby.

A stream of saliva issued from the Alsatian's mouth; his jaws were open, the large pink tongue curling forward, huge white teeth revealed.

"Just a minute more, my pets," Paula said. "Greedy boys, then."

Her voice was crooning. When she had finished preparing the bowls, she set them on the floor in a row. Each dog went to his own and sat before it, waiting to be told he might eat. Paula crossed to the back door, opened it, and went out to call the missing Labrador.

"Go on, my boys," she said to the others, returning, and waited by the open door till Boris padded in and went over to his own bowl.

Paula picked up the chicken, put it in a meat tin, opened the refrigerator and took out some dripping

27

wrapped in crumpled foil; she sniffed it, and then, with the knife she had used for the dogs' dinner, cut off a lump which she arranged on top of the bird. It slid off the slippery wet breast, so she picked it up in her fingers and wedged it over the bone. She wiped the knife across the thighs of the bird before putting it, unwashed, away in a drawer; the roasting tin went into the oven.

After this, Paula stood watching the dogs while they ate. Their jaws made a chumping, slopping sound. After some time another noise penetrated her consciousness: the crying of a child.

She ignored it for over ten minutes, but it grew louder and louder, and at last, exasperated, Paula went out of the kitchen and down the passage to what had once been a breakfast room. The floor was covered in dirty worn linoleum, and the room contained a cheap deal table, several unmatched chairs, a large marrow bone, gnawed white, a chewed-up rubber ball, and a child's cot in which a small girl, wearing only a sweater, stood up shaking the bars and crying hysterically. The blankets on which she stood were stained, and now they were saturated too.

"Damn you, you filthy little beast!" Paula put her two strong hands round the child's chest and plucked her from the cot. "This is what happens when dogs foul their beds," she said, and seizing the sodden blanket, she rubbed the child's contorted little face against the wet wool. Then she took the child, held face downwards under one arm, along the passage to the lavatory. It was quite bare except for the pan and washbasin. She thrust the child inside and closed the door upon her.

Paula's husband, Guy Curtis, ran an import and export business based in London, but he spent a great deal of time abroad, chiefly in South America.

He had met Paula at a party in London; he was between women at the time, and her muscular body, gaunt face and deepset brown eyes had intrigued him. He learned that she was a sculptor, but it was some time before he saw her work and realized that she was quite ungifted; at least, in his view. She turned out models of animals woodenly posed, which were cast by a middleman and sold to tourist shops as souvenirs; and she lived on a houseboat with her dogs. Without really meaning anything very much, he embarked on an affair with her and was trapped into marriage by the oldest trick of all. One of his friends warned him that she only wanted a permanent meal ticket and that was why she had let it happen, but Guy thought it was bad luck on any child to be born illegitimate. After their marriage they bought the house in Bidbury because it was convenient for London, had space for her animals, and a ready-made studio shed in the garden. The baby, when it arrived, was a thin listless little thing who cried a lot. Guy found her pathetic, and at the same time such attraction as Paula had held for him vanished, so most of the time he kept away. But he did not think seriously of ending the marriage legally; having a wife was a protection from other women who became too demanding. Laura grew from a crying baby into a whining, charmless little girl, and because she did not know him, she cried whenever they met.

Children were better not fussed, Guy thought, when he bothered to consider his daughter at all. He gave her mother a generous allowance and thought no more about his responsibility.

Lincoln Close, where Jamie Renshaw lived with his parents and small sister, was a small development of modern houses south of the square in Old Bidbury. To the north, New Bidbury had grown up round an industrial area with a modern shopping centre and colonies of housing estates. Next to the Renshaws lived the Armitages. Kenneth Armitage worked for a New Bidbury firm which made office equipment; he was an ambitious man, active in local affairs and now a councillor. Sarah Armitage was always behind with her household tasks because she got side-tracked by dipping into books, playing with her small son, Simon, or simply day-dreaming. She kept meaning to undertake something constructive, but the most she had managed was to enrol, this winter, in a weekly yoga class.

Among Kenneth's activities was bellringing, which he had done as a boy. In Old Bidbury the team practised every Wednesday evening for two hours, and sometimes they rang peals which lasted far longer, forcing those who lived near the church to turn up their radios, play their records loudly, and shut all the windows. Kenneth regarded this interest as a relaxation; his council work was his civic duty; his hobby was carpentry, and he attended an evening class in it one night a week. He was thus frequently out in the evening. Sarah's yoga meant that there was now another evening in the week when

30

she need not sit, tense and bad-tempered, with Kenneth. She was lonely when he was out, but she was uncomfortable when he was not.

This Sunday Kenneth had, as usual, rung the bells morning and evening, and in the evening for once he attended the service; he sat next to a nice-looking girl with a pleasant voice and had let his own reedy tenor go, hoping that she would admire it, but she'd given no sign.

When he got home, Simon was asleep, cold supper was laid in the dining recess, and Sarah was practising the shoulder stand upstairs in the bedroom.

Kenneth was annoyed not to find her eager for his return. He poured out two sherries and sat sipping his in the living area which was furnished with G-plan pieces and had Athena prints on the walls. Kenneth was well satisfied with the marks of material success around him, but less so with his wife, who was not living up to the expectations he had of her when he invited her to take up the post. His worldly ascent was assured, but what about her? He feared that Sarah would always be lagging behind.

He called up to her that her sherry was waiting, a note of asperity in his voice. What could she be doing?

Sarah, chin pressed into her chest, stared defiantly at her legs which were in the air. She was beginning to feel rather uncomfortable and would have to return to a more normal position soon, but she had decided to assert herself. She would not run meekly down just because he called: let him wait.

With luck there would be a good play on television, so that they need not try to communicate, for their conversations always became either arguments or instructional lectures from Kenneth.

Emptying her mind, in approved yoga fashion, she adopted the plough posture, feet touching the floor over her head, and stayed in the position some minutes.

She went down at last, past Gyp, the Airedale, who lay on the floor outside Simon's room, and when Kenneth asked what had delayed her she looked at him coldly.

"I was busy," was all she said.

Mrs Costello, after her lunch with Mrs Minter, had a nip of brandy when she got home, then a snooze. After that she let Pedro out into the garden and joined him there, weeding among the vigorous shoots which the bulbs were sending up. She was rather surprised to see a large, obviously male, footprint on the path by the gate to Lincoln Road, where the ground was damp and the grass worn thin so that only a few sprigs showed in the earth. Perhaps it was the mark of the dustman who had called on Thursday, she thought vaguely, and forgot about it, working on, kneeling on the ground, until dusk fell.

CHAPTER
FIVE

On the Monday morning after Emma's outing in the car, Madge arrived at the shop to find Norman outside it with a small boy.

"Ah — Madge," he said as soon as he saw her. "Go in, will you, please, and open up when it's time. I'll not be long," and with no further explanation he set off with the little boy down Funnel Lane.

Madge obediently went into the shop, snibbed the door shut behind her, and hung up her coat in the back lobby. She pulled down her new bright green sweater, bought specially to impress Norman but since it would be covered up all day unlikely to be noticed, and put on her clean overall. Then she set to, and was just ready at nine, the floor swept, the counter-top shining, to open the shop. She started to dust the stock next; trade was seldom brisk first thing on a Monday, though some travellers usually came that day. Norman soon reappeared.

"Mrs Widnes didn't call down, did she?" he asked.

"No," said Madge. "Shall I pop up?"

"I'll go," said Norman, "she wasn't too well in the night."

"Oh dear," said Madge, and watched him go upstairs.

That morning the Alsatian had once again deflected Jamie. When Norman took him past, it had stood watching, not even barking this time. No one could say it was vicious or menacing; it appeared almost indifferent. It was not even in the roadway, a danger to traffic; it was just alarming to look at, especially if you were rather small.

"Why don't you go and see Mrs Curtis about it?" Emma suggested when Norman told her that that he taken Jamie up the road again. "Ask her to keep it in."

"Perhaps I will. Or the kid's parents might." Norman was sponging her pale, clammy face. "Or I could offer to fix the fence for her. Though the gate is always open — if she closed that it might help to keep the dog in, fence or no fence."

"You let her mend her own fence, Norm," said Emma. "You've enough to do without that. Once start it, and you don't know where it would end. She might have you round there every five minutes." Emma did not trust what she knew of Paula Curtis.

"Now is that likely, dear?" Norman asked her. "As if I'd let her take advantage of me."

"You're softhearted," said Emma. And might be an easy target, she thought but did not say aloud.

Norman was not interested in analysing his own nature; he was more concerned with Emma's condition. From time to time she had turns like this, and there were pills she took. He gave her one, with a drink, and later that morning when he went up for his tea she seemed better.

Felicity was pleased to find Jamie punctual again; she knew nothing about Norman's part in this achievement for they had not met since the first time it happened. She had spent Sunday cleaning the flat and washing her hair, then scrutinizing advertisements for teaching posts abroad. The sensible thing was to put as many miles as possible between herself and Norman. He would manage perfectly well without her, or if he could not, would soon find somebody else.

Because she had nothing else to do and enjoyed singing, she went to church on Sunday evening, where, without knowing who he was, she sat next to Kenneth Armitage. During the sermon, which was exceedingly dull, she remembered the youths in the pub and their conversation and wondered again if she should tell the police what she had overheard. But by Monday she had forgotten it again.

Mrs Costello went to the laundrette on Monday as part of her weekly ritual. She took her washing in a large polythene bag and watched it spin round. It was a way of passing the time, although most people left to do other things while the machine ran.

Mrs Bowling came in and bundled the Widnes washing into one machine and her own into another, before bustling back to the shop. She was a brisk little woman, over sixty now but still energetic; her husband was a ticket collector at New Bidbury station.

"How's Mrs Widnes?" asked Mrs Costello, detaining her.

"Bit poorly today — she went out for a car drive yesterday and it was too much for her, poor soul," said

Mrs Bowling, who privately thought that Mrs Costello looked none too good either, though that might be due to the gin. Mrs Bowling knew she consumed a fair bit of it, for she often saw her coming away from the off-licence with a couple of bottles in her string bag. It must cost so much, Mrs Bowling thought; no wonder the old woman looked half starved — she couldn't be spending enough on food.

Mrs Costello hung her tumble-dried washing round the kitchen. Then she set off with Pedro to walk to New Bidbury, where she bought some knickers at Marks and Spencer's, red nylon ones with black lace edging at the knee. Next, she went to W.H. Smith's and looked at magazines. While she did this, Pedro kept getting his lead tangled among the other shoppers causing a good deal of exasperation. She bought two paperback thrillers and a biro; she was always losing them when she fell asleep over the *Daily Telegraph* crossword, but seldom thought of searching for them under the cushion of her armchair. Next she turned down a wide arcade that linked the big stores to a row of smaller shops, among them a health shop and the dry-cleaners. As she approached, she heard a child crying hysterically, and outside the cleaners she saw a small girl standing on the pavement sobbing in total despair. She was facing the cleaner's window, but she was too small to see over its solid base.

"Have you lost your mummy, dear?" asked Mrs Costello. She transferred Pedro's lead to the hand which held her shopping bag and took the child's hand with the other.

Immediately, the crying stopped.

"Is she in there? Your mummy? In the shop?" asked Mrs Costello.

But the child was unable to answer.

Mrs Costello thought of finding a policeman, but decided to make her own inquiries first. With difficulty, hung about as she was with child, shopping and dog, she opened the door of the cleaner's and said to a woman who stood by the counter, "Is this your little girl?"

"Yes — and you leave her alone," snapped Paula Curtis. "She's to wait outside. You mind your own business."

Mrs Costello, shocked, backed out of the shop. Inside, Mrs Pearce, Madge's mother, who was serving Paula, looked horrified.

The child began to cry again, and Mrs Costello bent down, dumping her bag, to console her. Pedro, stumpy tail wagging, stood by, displaying goodwill.

Paula came furiously out of the shop.

"I told you to leave her alone," she said, caught Laura roughly by the arm and dragged her away, scolding her loudly as they went. Mrs Costello stared after them, appalled; it took her a few minutes to gather herself together and go into the cleaner's with a shabby tweed skirt that needed their attentions.

Lydia Renshaw was always busy with dressmaking, running up curtains or chair-covers, making jewellery from bits of quartz, or other such projects. Her industry made Sarah Armitage, who lived next door, feel inadequate, but she was grateful for Lydia's friendship.

On Monday afternoon Sarah, Simon and Gyp, the Airedale, were all at the Renshaws. The smell of freshly baked bread filled the house, and now Lydia sat crocheting while Sarah, feeling decadent because idle, lounged in a large armchair. The two babies sat on the floor among bricks and toys playing solitary games in harmony together while their mothers talked. At least, Sarah supposed that they talked. They each, it was true, took turns to speak while the other listened, but Sarah felt they merely made sounds, not contact.

"I must be going round the bend," she thought distractedly when Lydia's voice suddenly ceased and it was her turn. What had Lydia been saying?

She uttered the first words that came into her head.

"Why don't you get a dog?"

Lydia looked rather surprised. She had been talking about organically grown vegetables and pure food, subjects dear to her heart. But she rallied.

"We mean to," she said. "It's important for the children."

Sarah knew that she needed Gyp for herself. When, as nowadays constantly happened, she found herself wondering what on earth she was doing living with a man who thought only of his status, civic affairs and bellringing, and for whom she felt nothing more than anxious impatience, it was Gyp who kept her in touch with reality. She'd had him long before she had Simon. Kenneth had never objected to him; it was proper to keep a dog — it rounded off the family circle of man, wife and two children, with pet by the hearth: that was his blueprint. Simon had obligingly arrived on schedule; it would soon be time, according to Kenneth's plan, to indent for his sister. What would happen if a brother arrived, Sarah wondered, or worse, no second child? Or wouldn't God dare to defy Kenneth?

"How did you meet Geoff?" she asked now.

Lydia hid her surprise at Sarah's inconsequentiality and crocheted on.

"I've always known him," she said. "We lived near each other."

"Oh. The boy next door."

"A mile away," said Lydia. "I never took much notice of him, though, till a tennis club dance."

She'd gone with someone else, and Geoffrey had suddenly revealed that he was jealous.

"Are you ambitious for him?" Sarah demanded. "I mean, do you want him to get on the board of his firm? Shall you have the boss to dinner?"

"Yes, yes, and yes," said Lydia. "Why do you ask?"

She thought that Sarah seemed very much on edge. Surely she wanted the same things for Kenneth?

"I just wondered if you ever got fed up," said Sarah.

"Why should I?" asked Lydia. "I've nothing to complain of."

The night before, Sarah and Kenneth had gone to bed not speaking. Her gesture of independence had misfired, for when she finally came downstairs she had knocked her sherry over. Kenneth, wearing a patient expression, had insisted on clearing up the mess and had cut himself on a piece of glass. He had said she was obviously in one of her clumsy moods. Then he had reminded her to put out a clean shirt for him in the morning and to check the buttons. She'd furiously demanded to know whether he had ever yet been left without a clean shirt or found one without a button missing, and had flung the pile of neatly folded shirts at him.

She was to blame for the row, and she had not apologized. She longed to pour all this out but feared that Lydia would not be sympathetic; besides, she must keep up the pretence that all was well at home: it ought to be, for she had everything a girl was supposed to want. To confess otherwise was to admit failure, and it was her failure, not Kenneth's.

"Where did you and Kenneth meet?" Lydia inquired.

"On holiday in Italy."

Kenneth had seemed different then, in his bright patterned shirt and blue shorts: he was lively and attentive. He showed her round churches and told her all about them; he was a good swimmer and encouraged her to be bolder. Translated back to England, he had seemed less attractive in his city suit, but he had continued to take her to art galleries and museums. They were free in England, she had noted at the time, and suppressed the reflection as base. After they married his instructions were concentrated on housekeeping matters and how she should mould herself to suit his own social and business aspirations. She often wondered now, why he had wanted to marry her when she was so far from his ideal, and could not know that at the age of thirty-three he had begun to fear no passable girl would accept him; he had pursued many a one, only to be snubbed in the end.

"How romantic," said Lydia. "And was he dashing and ardent?"

"I suppose so." Sarah had no great experience by which to judge.

"Keeping all that up would be very uncomfortable," said Lydia. "It doesn't last, does it? Friendship does."

"I suppose you're right," said Sarah.

But what if there was no friendship, and the ardour was all spurious?

"Where's Jamie?" she asked, to escape from such uncomfortable thoughts. "He's late, isn't he?" She liked Jamie, who often looked as worried as she constantly felt.

"Yes, he is, rather," said Lydia, seeming unconcerned. "I expect he's day-dreaming somewhere on the way home."

As she spoke, the back door opened. Jamie was trained to come in that way and change his shoes in the kitchen. In a few minutes he entered the room in his socks, carrying his sandals.

"Hullo, Jamie," said Sarah.

"Hullo," said Jamie hollowly.

His mother told him to put his sandals on, and he sat down on the floor to obey. That afternoon he had passed the Alsatian; it had meant loitering about until some more children came along Foster Avenue. He'd tagged on behind them and gone breathlessly past, but he still felt a bit sick with the fear he had felt.

Gyp looked up at him; his square face stared genially at Jamie as he put on his shoes. The snag about Mrs Armitage, who was otherwise one of Jamie's favourite people, was Gyp; but Jamie trusted her, and so he knew that Gyp would not bite him. I'm not really afraid of dogs, he told himself firmly, remembering his father's threat to buy one if he was. To prove himself, he went over to the hearth, put out a tentative hand, and gingerly patted Gyp's back. The dog gave him a perfunctory lick, then laid his head down again on his paws and resumed his staring session with the fire.

Only Sarah noticed Jamie's tense expression as he carried out this self-imposed challenge.

CHAPTER
SIX

After school that afternoon Felicity went to the shop. Norman immediately handed on to Madge the customer he was looking after and came over to her. His obvious pleasure at her made Felicity's resolution falter; she picked up a china mug and looked at the mark on its base.

"I want to talk to you," she began. The mug had been made in Stoke-on-Trent.

"I'm sorry about Saturday. It couldn't be helped," said Norman.

By this he took away the initiative. He was looking at her intensely; there was nothing abject about him.

"You've never met Emma, have you?" he asked. "She'll be having her tea now. Come on up."

"No — Norman, I couldn't!" Felicity was horrified.

But Norman had turned to Madge, who had finished with her customer.

"Mrs Widnes has got her tea, hasn't she, Madge?"

For every afternoon Madge went upstairs and made it for her.

"Yes, Mr Widnes. I took it to her ten minutes ago," said Madge. And had slipped her some custard cream biscuits from the hidden tin to reinforce the permitted slice of crisp-bread.

"I'm taking Miss Baxter up to see her," said Norman. "You carry on down here."

"Norman, no —" Felicity was still protesting, but in muted tones, because of Madge.

"Come along." Norman paid no heed, and swept her out of the shop. There was a lobby at the back, with the entrance to the store-room on the left, and on the right the narrow, steep staircase. "This way," Norman directed, propelling her before him.

"Norman, no! I didn't come for this," said Felicity, stopping halfway.

He put his hands on her waist. "I know. But it had to happen one day," he said.

She didn't agree, but he would not let her escape.

At the top of the stairs there was a long landing, off which led several doors. One was open.

"I'll go first," said Norman.

Why is he doing this, thought Felicity wildly, but she had no time to wonder any longer, for he had gone through the open door and it was beyond her to turn and flee. Her feet seemed to have become stuck to the patterned carpet on the landing.

"Oh, Norman, there you are," said a voice, none too clearly.

"Yes, dear. And I've brought a visitor. Miss Baxter from the school," Norman said. He turned to Felicity. "Come along in."

Like one hypnotized, Felicity obeyed.

The room she went into was quite large, with a good deal of furniture crammed into it: a dining table, several armchairs, a sideboard, and a huge sofa by the window

44

on which reclined a woman who looked as if she were made of lard. Tiny eyes were sunk in white folds of flesh; several chins rested on her chest so that she appeared to be neckless. A female Humpty Dumpty, Felicity thought hysterically, as she noticed the tiny feet in smart bronze patent shoes protruding from under a soft rug spread over Emma's legs. She's vain about her feet, Felicity registered. The ankles were covered: perhaps they were swollen.

Norman had crossed to the sofa and bent to kiss Emma's forehead. Over her head he looked compellingly at Felicity, who slowly stepped forward.

Emma stretched out a hand.

"How nice of you to call," she said regally.

Felicity took the extended hand and felt the limp touch of podgy fingers.

"Do sit down," said Emma. "Norman —" she waved a hand, still in queenly style, and Norman picked up the kettle. A tea-tray rested on a table close to Emma. Staring, unable to utter, Felicity watched Norman top up the teapot; she saw crumbs on a plate.

"I'll get a cup," said Norman, and he left the room.

Emma, with another imperious gesture, indicated a low chair that faced her, and Felicity sank slowly down upon it. Now that the situation confronted her, she was appalled.

"You've been at the school some time, Miss Baxter, haven't you?" Emma was saying. "I've seen you in the square. You've got a little red car. I know so many people by sight, but not to talk to. Though I did, of course, before I was ill."

Her voice was slightly slurred, and she spoke slowly, but there was no difficulty about understanding what she said.

"Three years," Felicity gasped, in reply.

"You like it? You'll be staying?"

Felicity plunged. "I like it, yes, but I plan to move soon," she said. "Probably overseas."

"I see." Emma nodded, and as Norman returned with a clean cup and saucer she said, "Miss Baxter tells me she's leaving soon to go abroad."

Norman set the cup steadily on the tray, poured out Felicity's tea and gave it to her. He hasn't asked if I take sugar, Felicity thought absurdly, so Emma will realize that he knows I don't. There was none on the tray.

She looked at Norman and then she looked at Emma, and she suddenly felt so icily cold that her teeth began to chatter. She clamped them together, accepting the cup and saucer from Norman and willing her hand to remain steady.

For Emma knew. Her acceptance showed on her face.

She's always known, Felicity realized. Perhaps not that it was me, but that there was someone. There had to be.

"I expect Bidbury gets a bit dull after a time," Norman said in an even voice.

"Not dull really. Limited," said Felicity.

She sipped her tea, calmer now. It was fantastic to be sitting here like this, with the pair of them. Norman had drawn up a chair for himself close beside his wife; he looked completely unperturbed.

"Norman likes children. He'd have made a good teacher. But he'd the shop coming to him," said Emma.

"And his mother needed him." She looked at Felicity. "Now he's saddled with me. And we've no family."

All the time she spoke the two beady eyes watched Felicity closely. It's as if I were an insect on a pin, and she was devising ways to torment me, thought the girl.

"Don't talk like that, dear," Norman said. "You know I regret nothing — nothing at all — except about your health, of course," and he laid his hand on Emma's arm, pressing it. She held up her plump hand and he clasped it firmly.

Felicity felt rather sick.

He loves her, she thought, half in horror, half fascinated.

"I went out for a drive yesterday," Emma said, in a lighter tone. She had proved her point.

"How nice," said Felicity.

"It was. But to do it again, we'd need the fire brigade," said Emma and laughed. Her fat body shook, huge breasts wobbling above the rug drawn over her knees. "I got stuck on the stairs."

"Well, here you are," said Felicity feebly.

"Yes."

For ten terrible minutes more Felicity sat there, making small talk. At one point Norman left them, to see if all was well below with Madge, and while he was gone Emma remarked on how good he was.

"He was broken up when his mother died," she said. "It was a mercy, though, when it happened. She'd suffered so much."

And Emma had moved in just when Norman was at his most vulnerable, Felicity thought. Why had they married? An affair, yes — but to marry him, with nearly twenty years between them, the wrong way round — it was obscene.

As if she could read her thoughts, Emma said "I wasn't always like, this, you know. That's me over there," and she nodded towards a photograph that stood on a bookcase across the room.

Felicity, still mesmerized, went over to look at it. It showed Norman looking plumper than he did now; and his hair, which had begun to recede, was quite thick. Beside him was an extremely good-looking woman who, even in a black-and-white photograph, looked full of vitality.

"It was lucky the stroke didn't kill me, wasn't it?" Emma said softly. "Or don't you think so?"

Felicity did not have to answer, for Norman came back then, but Emma would not let her leave yet. She began to ask about her work.

"Has Norman told you about Jamie Renshaw?" Emma asked.

"No. How could he have?" Felicity seized her chance to strike back in her own defence. "What about Jamie?"

"He's afraid of an Alsatian he meets in Foster Avenue on his way to school."

Felicity looked at Norman and saw him nod.

"Yes — it's true. He's been avoiding the dog by coming this way, up Funnel Lane and round by the main road," he said.

"Norman discovered what was happening and has taken Jamie past the Alsatian a couple of times," Emma said.

"So that's why Jamie's been late so often," Felicity exclaimed.

"The dog's quite gentle. But he does look rather fierce," Norman said.

"Norman can't bear anyone to be unhappy," said Emma. "He tries to please everyone."

Mrs Costello could not get the thought of the wailing child outside the cleaner's shop out of her mind. So upset was she that she went straight round to tell Mrs Minter about the incident.

Mrs Minter was making marmalade.

"I don't see what you can do about it now, Jane," she said, slicing rind. "You don't know who the woman was, do you?"

"No. She was like a harpy — hair all over the place and one of those shaggy coats, all fronded," said Mrs Costello colourfully. "As a matter of fact, I had the feeling I'd seen her before, but I don't know where."

Mrs Minter was appropriately shocked at the tale, but she also welcomed the chance of a crusade for Mrs Costello; it would be a positive action, and might deflect her from the gin on which she spent so much of her meagre income.

"You might see her again, if you keep a look-out," she said. "If you see anything else like that, perhaps you could report her to the police or the NSPCC."

"Yes, I could," agreed Mrs Costello. "Well, I do go into New Bidbury quite often — I go to the library twice a week, not to mention the fish shop." For frozen fish was the only sort obtainable in Old Bidbury and Pedro liked cod's heads, as a change from Meatimix. "I'll remember."

"That's right," said Mrs Minter encouragingly. "Good luck."

"You want to get rid of me," said Mrs Costello.

"I don't, but I must write some letters this evening and I want to get the marmalade done first," said Mrs Minter. "You're welcome to stay and chat to me while it boils. I'll make some tea."

But Mrs Costello was feeling the need for something stronger than tea, so she went away.

"That your old man's?" asked Harry Pearce, picking up a man's jacket on a wire hanger and still in the cleaner's plastic bag.

"Yes. One of the dogs got hold of it," said Paula Curtis. In fact Guy had thrown the garment out, and she had adopted it to wear herself.

"Mm. Thin fellow, isn't he?" Harry remarked, holding it against his own burly torso. He wondered if Edna had dealt with her at the cleaner's. The thought amused him: two more different women you couldn't find — Edna so neat, rather prim, and utterly virtuous; Paula as crude as any man.

"Fed the dogs, have you?" he asked.

"Can't you tell? Look at them."

They lay about the kitchen, replete; the bulldogs asleep; Alsatian immobile but all the time watching the humans; the others dreaming, whimpering now and then.

"What about the kid?"

50

"She's off too. Hours ago. She never wakes."

She did, but far off in Paula's bedroom they would not hear her.

"Come on, then. What are we waiting for."

He pushed her before him upstairs. It was a bit of luck, this one, coming just as he'd tired of his last little sideline, which was how he described them to himself. He'd never met anything like Paula before. There had been plenty of others, and there would be more, he hoped; getting about as he did in his van all over the district he met lonely and frustrated women often enough, though not all of them, however desperate, gave him the nod. It was never worth pressing, however much you fancied them. But this one was different. He never thought he'd go for a slut — and she was one, for all she called herself a sculptor, making clay models in her shed in the garden. She was wild; and though he knew, obscurely, that it wouldn't last for long, at the moment he couldn't get enough of her.

When he went home that night, Edna, who seldom took any notice now when he got back so late, stirred as he slid into bed beside her.

"Where have you been, Harry?" she mumbled. "Petting some dog? You smell of it."

She was a bitch. Edna was right.

Every Monday, after taking her dachshunds for their early morning walk round the streets, Rose Hallam spent the morning scouring the house from top to toe. Privately her husband Bob, who was manager of a bank in New

Bidbury, wished she were less perfect a housekeeper; he felt guilty if a speck of mud fell from his shoe to the pale carpet, or if he did not put away a book he had been reading. But Rose never nagged; it was just a compulsion.

Since she'd taken on her new job at Marguerite's, a boutique in the town, she'd been better, however; he'd once actually noticed a film of dust she'd missed along a picture and had exulted. She was happier now, but he wished she could come out from behind the barrier of her shyness and make friends of her own. He was by nature, cheerful and gregarious; he enjoyed golf, which he often played at weekends but he felt guilty at leaving Rose alone then. She depended on him for companionship, and for attracting other people to them both. The little dogs were something he suffered in silence. He loved Rose, and so he understood her need to croon over them as if they were human babies, but the fact that she needed them so much made him feel that he had failed her.

"Well — seen anyone today?" he asked, kissing her, when he came home on Monday evening.

"I talked to Sarah Armitage," said Rose. "We met when I was out with my boys for their walkies."

Bob tried not to wince at how she said this.

"That's good," he remarked.

"I don't think she's very happy," said Rose. "She seems rather nervy."

"Oh darling, surely she's all right," said Bob. The Hallams were older than the Armitages and the Renshaws, and lived in a larger, more expensive house; they were barely acquainted. Bob knew, however, about

Kenneth Armitage's bank account and his modestly comfortable position. "They've got a nice house — young Armitage will do well."

"That isn't everything," said Rose. "Kenneth may be the trouble. He's got a mean look — and he's smug. I wonder if he's kind."

Bob felt unable to answer this, and was anyway not much interested in the Armitages' matrimonial relationship, although pleased that Rose seemed to have made some sort of friendly contact with Sarah.

"What's for dinner?" he asked, and the Hallams settled down to a tranquil evening with sherry before their meal, *Panorama* on television, and then a game of backgammon, which they had recently taken up.

That evening after leaving the shop, Madge had just crossed the square when a figure loomed at her from the kerbside: Mick Green, one of her brother Reg's friends.

"Hi, Madge," he said.

"Hi yourself," said Madge, who had no time for Mick.

"Like a lift? I've got the bike." Mick owned a powerful motorbike.

"No, thanks."

"You scared?"

"Course I'm not scared."

"Well, then."

"I'd rather walk."

"Stuck up, are we?"

"In a hurry."

"Get on the bike, then."

"No."

"I'm going round your way. Going to see Reg."

"He won't be home yet."

"Yes, he will. Gets home same time I do. Come on, Madge."

"No," said Madge, and she pushed past him, hurrying towards the bus stop.

"Get you," Mick said to her retreating back. He knew few other girls who would refuse such an invitation. But then most girls weren't like Madge.

He wanted to ask her where the money was kept overnight in Widnes' Stores. He'd thought she'd be easy.

He'd have to find some other way to get the information out of her.

CHAPTER
SEVEN

Every morning now, Jamie came into the square, and Norman, watching for him, suspected that he no longer went to Foster Avenue first; but anyway the Alsatian was always there.

On Thursday, when Jamie had run on to school, Norman turned in at Paula Curtis's gate.

The Alsatian followed him up the drive; it began to growl softly, then to bark. Norman felt slight apprehension but walked resolutely on, and then a black Labrador approached. It snuffled and snorted at him waving its tail and lifting its lip in a sort of grin. More noisy barking began as the bulldogs joined in, and the collie tore round the side of the house towards him.

The uproar was fearful, and Norman was relieved when Paula appeared, calling the dogs to order. They fell back, the collie, hackles up, crouching beside her, snarling.

"Mrs Curtis — sorry to intrude," Norman said. "Er — have you managed to mend your fence yet?"

"No — there's no hurry for it. It's been down for months," said Paula.

"Er — your dog — it's always in the road," Norman said. "This one." He pointed to the Alsatian.

"Hector? Yes, he does wander," said Paula. "But the fence makes no difference — it's the one next to Oak House, that's empty, which is broken. Hector goes out of the gate."

As her gate was almost permanently open it was only surprising that the whole pack wasn't out in the road, Norman thought.

"Some of the children going to school are afraid of him," he said.

"Lord — he wouldn't hurt a fly," said Paula. "He practically shares Laura's cot. I shut the others in the orchard. Tell the kids not to be so silly."

"Could you keep him in till the children have passed?" Norman asked.

"I could try, but I won't remember," Paula said.

Norman had to leave it at that. It was really up to Jamie's parents to complain, but if the dog had hurt no one it was probably impossible to compel Mrs Curtis to keep him in; each dog was allowed his bite, in law.

He went back to the shop feeling somewhat defeated and wondering what would happen if the collie got out; it had looked really vicious.

After the shop closed at one o'clock he went off on his usual weekly errands, hurrying through them so that he would arrive before Felicity at her flat. What she had said to Emma about going abroad was just talk: she couldn't have meant it, he told himself. But how long could things go on like this? There must be an end.

He caught himself up. Such thoughts were forbidden. He had tried not to admit them as he watched his mother dwindle away, and Emma was not dwindling. She was becoming not only physically larger but emotionally more demanding. Sometimes he hated her for her encroachment on his freedom.

But he deserved to pay some price, after all.

He could see that last drink of his mother's as if it had just been prepared: her invalid food, a sort of predigested gruel, and mixed into it all those pills — the blue cases pulled off and the powder stirred in with the sugar. She'd said it tasted very bitter, and had screwed up her face, but she had swallowed it. He had almost hoped she would vomit it up, but she hadn't.

Next day she was dead.

He had married Emma at once. Spouses could not give evidence against one another, if anyone should ever ask about that night.

But nobody did.

Madge did not like Thursdays, for then she was parted from Norman for the afternoon. On the other hand it gave her a chance to wash her hair and apply a face-pack attack to her acne without risk of ridicule from her brother. Her mother was at home then, too, for the cleaner's was also closed; she used the time to bake and clean, and often Madge helped, but this week she decided to go shopping in Muddington, twelve miles away, where early closing was on Wednesday and the market was held on Thursday. Her new green sweater didn't go too well with her jeans, and she planned to get some matching trousers.

She caught the two o'clock bus and was in Muddington market before three, strolling among the stalls. She did not see Mick Green as he followed her to the bus stop, and she did not see him at Muddington when she got off the bus. He had travelled faster on his motor-bike. She did not notice him following her round the market, either.

He had decided that this might be a better way to spend the afternoon than at his bench in the factory.

Norman's calls took longer than he expected and Felicity was home before he arrived. It had been raining, and her wet raincoat hung on a peg inside the door, making him aware of her live presence before he saw her.

Her hair, where it had escaped from her scarf, was damp.

"How did you get so wet?" he asked, holding her.

"I had to walk home — the car wouldn't start," she said. "Jack Phelps is going to fix it — it must be the damp."

Norman was reminded sharply of the first time he had come here, when again it had rained and her car had been in dock. He held her closer, but Felicity pushed him away. She must, today, make him realize that she meant what she had said to Emma, but the moment he touched her she felt herself weaken. She could not understand why he had this power; he was nothing to look at — thin, sandy-haired, not much taller than she was, and when she analysed their relationship she knew that it was their loneliness which had, in the beginning, drawn them together; yet they had shared rapture, even love.

It would be difficult to leave him.

He had brought éclairs for tea, and produced them now, in a paper bag. They had got slightly squashed and the cream was splurging out.

"I got these — I love them," said Norman.

"And you can never have them at home because they'd be bad for Emma. I know," said Felicity in a bitter voice.

"Darling, that's unkind," Norman protested.

"Do you expect me to be kind, after what you did on Monday?" Felicity snapped, giving way to her angry resentment. "That was a filthy trick to play, taking me to see her."

"She enjoyed it. She doesn't meet many people," Norman said.

"And what about me? I didn't enjoy it at all — I felt terrible," stormed Felicity. "But I don't matter, do I?"

"Oh, Felicity, you do — you mean the world to me," cried Norman. "But you've seen Emma now — you've seen the sort of life she has — be generous."

He tried to put his arms around her again, but Felicity angrily pushed him away.

"You love her," she accused. "I could tell that you do, seeing you with her."

Before, she had never let herself consider such a possibility. She had convinced herself that Norman, in a mad moment of folly, unbalanced after the strain of his mother's illness and death, had been ensnared by a much older woman who had wanted him because of the security offered by his thriving business.

"She needs me," Norman temporized.

"Of course she does. You're her life-line. And you're wonderful with her. But it isn't hard for you — you're so kind-hearted, I know you are — you couldn't be cruel to — to a wasp," said Felicity wildly. "But you're cruel to me."

"Yes I am." Norman's whole body suddenly sagged with dejection. "I'm cruel to visit you like this, hole-in-the-corner, when you deserve so much more."

"Oh —" Felicity raised both her hands in the air. "That's not cruel — I went into this with my eyes open — no — you're cruel because —"

"Because I don't love only you," Norman said quietly. "Because I'm tied to a fat, ageing woman, and not just by duty. But I hate touching her, Felicity. God help me, but I find her repulsive now."

He could barely utter the treacherous words.

Now, he had said, qualifying the statement. It was through Emma that he had learned how to bring delight as a lover, and she still wanted him to touch her. With icy clarity Felicity knew the truth.

Later, in bed, Norman said: "You won't really leave, will you?"

Felicity, with her face against his shoulder, would not waver.

"Yes, I will, Norman," she said. "As soon as I can."

But Emma might die: what then? Had he thought of that? She looked ill enough for anything to happen.

"No," he was saying. "No, I won't let you."

"What does the doctor say about Emma?" Felicity asked, turning her face away from him.

She had a right to be answered.

"Her heart's not too good," Norman said. "She could have another stroke at any time. But she could live for years. She's not in any pain — she doesn't suffer at all."

"She does. She knows about us," said Felicity.

Norman drew back from her, shocked.

"Oh no, it's impossible," he said.

"She does. I could tell. She's clever — she knew I hated meeting her. She spends her life watching other people — she saw we weren't just acquaintances. She must have suspected you had someone, Norman. She guessed it was me. Perhaps you meant her to — perhaps that's why you took me up there. To demonstrate your power over both of us. Perhaps you are cruel after all. You meant to hurt us both."

"I never want to hurt Emma," Norman said. "She must never, never suffer."

CHAPTER
EIGHT

Two-year-old Laura Curtis was accustomed to being thrust into the garden while her mother was working. She would trot round the shrubbery, sometimes getting lost but finding her way back to the house in the end. She cried a lot, because she was hungry, or because she had fallen over, or was cold; but no one ever came to see what was wrong and she usually stopped from exhaustion. Sometimes she played, lethargically, with a stick or some stones. She had no toys. Boris, the labrador, usually pottered about near her. She was used to the dogs, accepting them as part of her daily surroundings; they licked her impartially as if she were a puppy belonging to all of them, and none, not even the collie, had ever snapped at her or hurt her. But Boris was the one she loved; she would cling to him, arms wrapped round his neck, and one day when she saw him disappear through the broken fence adjoining the house next door it was natural for her to follow.

The garden seemed much the same as her own, though in fact it was wilder, with tangled shrubs and uncut grass. She and Boris wandered about in it contentedly; no one disturbed them. Her mother, in her studio shed, did not know where they were. There was a pond beyond what had once been lawn, and Boris drank some of the water from it; Laura squatted beside him, holding on to his coat, peering in. She saw herself reflected, and saw also a fat goldfish swim from under a lily leaf and then vanish again.

When Boris padded back to the gap in the fence, she followed.

Lydia Renshaw believed in experiencing life as richly as possible, and at all levels. Her creed included keeping Geoffrey in mint condition, so far as she could, in order that he should fulfil himself at work and at home. She fed him on wholesome food, was ready whenever he was at home to discuss politics, their children, or any other theme, and performed with conscientious energy in bed.

She was physically robust, had conceived and borne Jamie without any trouble, and had been chagrined that it took her five years to become pregnant again. However, now that she had Claire there was no possible ground for any self-reproach. When Geoff got his next rise they would move out of town and notch up another rung climbed. She played badminton one night a week and went to upholstery class on another. Geoffrey would not take up any evening classes, not even a language course; he liked reading and listening to records, and willingly stayed in with the children whenever she went out. She had recently taken up bridge, and he encouraged this too, though refusing, for his own part, to follow her lead. Each maintained that the other should be free to develop as an individual; they worked at their marriage with enthusiasm. Or Lydia did, and Geoff submitted; she never suspected with what relief he saw her depart for her various activities, knowing that for two hours or so he need make no effort to keep pace with her.

On Thursday afternoon she went to post a letter, and met Mrs Costello out walking with her spaniel.

"Well, Claire!" Mrs Costello bent over the pram and loomed at the baby, who looked startled at this sudden red face appearing, but did not cry. "Aren't you getting a big girl, then?"

Claire was too young to reply, and Mrs Costello, swept on, saying "May I walk a little way with you, Lydia?"

Mrs Costello tended to tag on to people she met when out for a stroll. Lydia, who had experienced this before, felt a glow of virtue at being consciously kind to a lonely old lady as she agreed. Before they had gone far together, Mrs Costello had related the tale of the wailing child outside the cleaner's, satisfactorily horrifying Lydia.

"But I don't know who she is — the mother," said Mrs Costello as they walked past the end of Paula Curtis's garden.

"She must live in New Bidbury," said Lydia. "She couldn't come from round here." Old Bidbury parents, the inference was, were too enlightened for such conduct.

Mrs Costello, however, believed that people could batter babies anywhere.

That evening, Mrs Minter went to see Mrs Costello. She found her sitting by the gas-fire with a half-empty glass beside her and the television on. Mrs Costello turned the sound down but let the picture flicker on.

As usual, exasperation at her friend's lack of order filled Mrs Minter. The small room was crammed with large pieces of furniture which had come from Mrs Costello's former home and which she refused to sell in spite of her impoverished plight, though some were quite valuable. They were part of her, she said, and she could not bear to be separated from them.

"You could get smaller pieces which would fit into the and have cash over," said Mrs Minter. "I'd help you to get the best prices."

But Mrs Costello stubbornly refused. Mrs Minter still hoped to make her change her mind, and raised the subject whenever Mrs Costello was in fair spirits, which seemed to be less and less often. Tonight the older woman looked very gaunt, sitting in a huddled posture, and somewhat sozzled by now. She had lost a lot of weight recently. Widowhood was not easy for her, but it was not only the loneliness; she felt guilt too, and it would never quite wear off. She had met Charles Costello just after the first war; they had fallen in love, married, and had some golden years. Their two sons were killed in the second war and things had never been quite right after that, although Jane Costello had not realized just how wrong they were. If she had, perhaps Charles might still be alive.

Mrs Minter accepted her own widowed state more robustly, though she sometimes wondered whether, if Hugh had lived, they would have grown bored with one another by now. Their few years together had been happy; he had been killed at the very end of the war, stepping on a mine when her son Derek was just a few months old. She had never found anyone else she could contemplate seeing every day for the rest of her life.

This evening, when she had refilled her own glass and given Mrs Minter some sherry, Mrs Costello disclosed that she had something on her mind.

"I met Lydia Renshaw today," she said. "I told her about that little girl I saw crying outside the cleaners in New Bidbury — you remember, Kitty."

"Yes."

"Lydia didn't know who she was."

"How could she? She didn't see her." Really, Jane could be exceedingly stupid at times; her brain must be atrophying from too much alcohol.

"True." Mrs Costello got up and wavered across the room to the table where she kept her drink readily available. "Drink up, Kitty, and have another," she said, pouring herself some more gin.

"One's quite enough for me," said Mrs Minter in a prissy tone. "I must go. What are you having for supper, Jane?"

"Oh — I shan't bother about it," said Mrs Costello. "I'm not hungry."

"Don't be silly. You must have something. I suppose you've run out of food again," said Mrs Minter, and went bossily out into the kitchen to look.

There was a slice of stale bread in a bin, a cube of dried cheese, a bottle of milk and two eggs in the refrigerator. In the larder she found a small tin of baked beans and six large ones of dog food. There were also two tomatoes. What could be done about this? She could not undertake to feed Jane Costello every day. However, tonight she would. She went back to the sitting-room carrying Mrs Costello's sheepskin coat.

"I see you've got plenty for Pedro and nothing for yourself as usual, Jane," she said. "Come along. I've got some home-made soup and pâté."

"I don't want anything," Mrs Costello protested, but in the end she gave in. Mrs Minter had to wait while Pedro was fed, and they left him behind, tucking in heartily to his jellied lumps of Meatimix.

A shaft of light showed between the curtains of the flat above Widnes' Stores as the two women crossed the square.

"It's Mrs Bowling's night there. They play cards every Thursday while Norman's out," said Mrs Costello. "I wonder where he goes? Round the pubs, do you think?"

"I've no idea," said Mrs Minter shortly. She would utter aloud no surmise about Norman's extramural activities.

"How sad it is," said Mrs Costello. "I don't know how he manages. It must have been so dreadful for him seeing his mother in that state. I've often wondered if he helped her on her way. She died so suddenly, in the end. Perhaps Emma knew, and he had to marry her to make her keep quiet."

Mrs Minter stopped abruptly in the middle of the road and looked at her friend's face, haggard in the light from the street-lamps.

"Jane, what a thing to say!" she exclaimed.

"It could be so," Mrs Costello insisted, swaying slightly. "I'm telling you, Kitty, most murders happen at home. It's well known."

"You read too many thrillers."

For Mrs Costello got through several every week.

"It could have happened," she repeated. "The papers are full of such things. I wouldn't blame him. There must have been plenty of drugs in the place — an extra big dose would do it, and no one would ever suspect."

Such an idea had never crossed Mrs Minter's mind.

"I hope you don't talk like this to anyone else," she said sternly. "It's slanderous."

"Perhaps he'll kill Emma one day," said Mrs Costello, unperturbed.

Madge had spent nearly an hour that afternoon wandering round Muddington's market looking at garments hung on rails, trying on coats she had no intention of buying, and examining slacks. She inspected cheap jewellery laid out on trestles and lockets on chains that swung from hooks, bought an apple and ate it, and finally drifted into the town itself where there were several shops selling clothes geared to the teenage market, in dark caverns with pop music blaring loudly. There were few trousers wide enough to contain her splendid hips and thighs, for most were cut to fit androgynous shapes with minimal flesh, but at last she found a pair which, by holding her breath in tightly, she could just zip up over her stomach; once inside, she had the fashionable poured-in look.

She paid for them, and as she left the shop with her parcel it began to rain. There was half an hour before her bus left, so she went to a café and bought a cup of tea and a large Danish pastry. The place was frequented mainly by young people; a juke-box played, and the air was hot and steamy, the smell of sweat mingling with the damp as more people came in for shelter off the street. Madge had been there only a few minutes when a youth pushed through the cluster of people at the counter and squeezed against the girl sitting opposite to her, forcing her to make room for him.

"Do you mind?" said the girl, but she moved up.

"Hi, Madge, how's things?" said Mick Green.

Madge looked at him over her cup of tea and did not reply.

"Having a nice afternoon are you?" Mick asked her cheerily.

Still no reply.

"Aren't you pleased to see me, then?"

Madge deliberately set down her cup, picked up her pastry and took a large bite. She chewed steadily, looking all round the room — anywhere but at Mick, with his impudent grin and piercing blue eyes. It did not occur to her that their meeting was not accidental; she just wished he would go away; perhaps he would if she ignored him.

"How's Reg?" he asked.

Madge finished her mouthful, turned her gaze upon him, and said austerely, "If you was at work, like you ought to be, then you'd know."

"Oh — I felt like a day off," said Mick airily. "Doesn't do to be a slave to routine. That's what you are, aren't you? A slave to that birk, Widnes."

Madge was stung to defence of her beloved.

"I'm not a slave. I work proper hours, and get paid regular, and Mr Widnes is ever so kind," she said.

"Tied, isn't he, with his missus like that?"

Madge would not answer.

"Don't you want me to talk to you?" Mick asked her. He turned to the unknown girl beside him, put his hand on his chest, and adopted a mournful expression. "She's breaking my heart," he declared.

The girl giggled.

"Get on," she said.

If she hung about, and the spotty-faced cow opposite went on like this, maybe he'd give up and make a play for her instead.

"It's the truth. I've been following her round all the afternoon waiting for a chance to talk to her, and now she won't let me."

Could it be true? Boys had followed Madge before, but only to mock her, and usually with their mates in attendance, spitting with laughter. Not boys like Mick, though. He could take his pick of girls; he would not waste time chatting her up if he didn't want to.

Madge had no cause to suspect Mick of any motive other that the obvious one: he wanted a bit of fun. She had been treating her pimples and trying at intervals to diet away some of her fat, mainly to be a worthier handmaid to Norman. Could it be that her efforts were succeeding and that she had acquired whatever mysterious attribute it was that she had previously lacked? Madge was no exception to the generalization that within every ugly duckling lurks a hidden swan. Her prickly resistance began to crack. Mick, accustomed to girls, noticed the slight flush on her pallid face and saw the absent-minded way she laid down her half-eaten pastry.

"Have another of those, Madge," he said. "I'll have one too. I'll be back," and he got up to go to the counter.

Madge thought about leaving while he was gone, but suppose he meant what he'd said? She would like to be certain.

"Don't you fancy him?" the other girl asked, curious.

"No," said Madge bluntly, but was not sure that it was exactly true. A rather odd feeling was going through her, such as she had experienced sometimes in the cinema during emotional scenes. It was not a sensation Norman's proximity ever aroused; her passion for him was utterly chaste: he was remote, on a pedestal, untouchable, sanctified.

Mick had gambled that Madge would remain. He returned with a plate of cream cakes, his own tea and another cup for her. It was rather like treating a kid, he thought, putting the bait down before her.

He asked about the shop, and what she did all day, and where the stock was kept, how many doors there were to the premises and if Norman went out much, skilfully inserting the questions among remarks about what was in her parcel and the current pop scene, and playing her choice on the juke-box. The other girl acknowledged defeat and left, baffled by Mick's apparent liking for the dough-faced girl. When she had gone, Mick drew his chair forward and engaged Madge's sturdy legs between his under the table. The funny feeling hit her again. It was nice, in a frightening sort of way, but she still did not trust Mick, and when he asked how much the shop took in cash she clammed up.

"Don't be so nosey, Mick," she said. "It's none of your business."

"Sorry, I'm sure," said Mick. "I was just interested," and he rubbed his leg against hers.

Madge was flustered. She had hitherto dodged the odd groper, and had never understood why other girls spent so much time thinking about sex. Surprise and excitement outran her alarm. She did not approve of Mick, but she did not know why; now she discovered the charm of a rogue. Madge was seldom the recipient of another person's undivided attention; Norman, in the shop, sometimes gave it to her, and so did Emma, and in her gauche way she returned their interest with simple loyalty. Now Mick, whom some would describe as a good-looking youth, was concentrating on her and her slow response began.

When she discovered that while they were talking the bus had gone, and Mick suggested the cinema, her protestations were quickly overcome.

While Madge was with Mick Green, Paula Curtis was out in her studio. The bulldogs, the collie and the Alsatian were with her, called in from the orchard where they had been roaming. They lay in a semi-circle on the floor, heads on paws, while she built clay up on a wire frame, making the foundation for a new model of the Alsatian's head. She worked at the clay, moulding it with her strong thumbs, the shed warm from a convector heater turned full on.

In the corner of the studio there was a divan piled with cushions and a rather grubby purple blanket; here, Paula lounged and smoked when she was resting.

Harry Pearce saw the light on in the shed and came there to her. The divan smelled faintly of dog, he noticed. It did not put him off.

In the house, Laura cried herself to sleep at last, and Boris, the Labrador, lay outside the door of her room.

CHAPTER
NINE

Jamie knew that at seven years old he should need no
escort to school. However, he had an idea and he put it
to Norman as soon as they were on their way the next
morning.

"If I had a bike, I could ride past that dog, very fast,"
he said.

"Well — maybe you could. But you haven't got one,
have you?"

"No. But it's my birthday soon. I might be given one.
I could try asking," said Jamie.

"They cost a lot," Norman pointed out.

"Everything does," said Jamie with a worldly air.

"Your dad might pick up a secondhand one, I suppose.
But I wonder if you'd be allowed one — there's a fair bit
of traffic round this way now."

"I'd ride very carefully," said Jamie earnestly.

"Well — no harm asking," said Norman.

They passed the Alsatian, and Jamie ran on up the
road while Norman went back to the shop, smiling to
himself. He enjoyed their meetings, though there was
really no need for them; but dogs did turn savage
sometimes, and children had been attacked. Norman

meant to ask Felicity to speak to Jamie's parents about the problem, but the need to make her change her mind about leaving Bidbury had driven it out of his head. And he hadn't succeeded in persuading her. She'd go, meet someone else, marry, have kids and forget him. For her happiness, it was what ought to happen, but he could not bear to think of it.

He was preoccupied with his own affairs when he returned to the shop and did not notice Madge's pallor, nor the fact that she would not look him in the eye. It was Emma who pointed out, later in the day, that Madge was not herself.

After the cinema, Mick had taken Madge to a pub and bought her vodka and lime; she liked its innocent taste and drank several without any coaxing. They had sat in the back row at the cinema, and before long Mick had distracted her attention from the screen; his roving hand excited her until her normal common sense dissolved. The idea she had of him was all wrong, she decided, clinging to his arm as they walked down the street.

Mick wondered how he would live this down with his friends, one or two of whom had seen him with Madge and made a few cracks about reject models and so forth, which Madge, if she heard, failed to understand. His behaviour in the cinema was automatic; it was what you went there for; but he knew now how Madge could be made to help him win his bet.

She was too young to be legally drinking in the pub, and it added to her reckless feeling. When she was really giggly they left, and Mick took her, on the back of his bike, to Muddington sports ground, where he knew from past experience that they should be safe from disturbance behind the pavilion. The cold air sobered Madge up slightly, and when he backed her up against the wall and it became clear what would happen, she was frightened. She struggled quite hard, but he told her it was too late now. Afterwards, frantically pulling her jeans round her trembling body, she turned to run off, but he caught hold of her.

"How do you think you'll get home? The last bus has gone," he said. "I'll take you on the bike."

Madge felt dirty, and she wanted to get away from him as fast as she could, yet his grasp on her arm, though firm, was not unkind.

"It's never all that good the first time," he said, for he saw that she was shaking. He wanted her brought low, so that she would do as he said, but he had expected to achieve this by binding her to him physically for as long as was necessary. Her obvious shock and distress surprised him, but he did not interpret it as an affront to his powers; it was merely the result of her being such a silly kid.

She felt so sore that she wondered whether she would be able to mount the bike, but she did, and was obliged to cling to him as they roared out of the town. He stopped at a lorry-driver's café on the main road and bought coffee for both of them.

"Can't take you home in that state," he said. "What'd your mum say?" Besides, he had not finished with her.

Madge drank the coffee and felt a little better. She could not look at Mick and she thought that everyone in the café would know exactly what had happened just by looking at her.

He sent her out to the washroom, and she washed her tear-stained face and her hands at the chipped basin. She could do nothing about the rest of herself until she got home. There was no escape from Mick; she couldn't walk to Bidbury, and as it was, by this time of night her mother would be doing her nut because she was not back.

Mick had washed and tidied himself too. His crisp curls were in place and he was talking to the blonde behind the counter when Madge appeared. He'd got two more cups of coffee.

"That Norman Widnes, where you work," he said. "Where's he keep his cash?"

Madge did not answer.

"I asked you a question. Where does he keep his money?" Mick demanded.

"In the bank," said Madge, in a mumbling voice.

"I mean his day's takings. When he empties the till. He doesn't leave it full at night, I'm sure. Where does he put it?"

"I don't know."

"Has he got a safe?"

No reply.

"You haven't seen one?"

Madge had first noticed the large steel box in Emma's wardrobe when she fetched her best pair of bronze court shoes from it at Emma's request. She set her lips firmly and did not answer.

"I asked you if you'd seen a safe," Mick repeated.

"No," said Madge. "Perhaps there isn't one."

But she was not a good enough dissembler; Mick was not deceived. He said no more then, but he stopped the bike when they were out in the country and took her into a field, and he did not let her alone until she had told him.

Afterwards, she vomited, and Mick, disgusted, had to wait until she had recovered somewhat before he could take her home. He told her mother she must have eaten something that disagreed with her, for she'd been ever so sick; he was sorry they were so late, but he'd been looking after her, and wasn't it lucky they'd met?

Mrs Pearce who had been worried almost out of her mind because Madge was so late, ended up by thanking him for being so thoughtful. Madge's father, who might have guessed that things were not quite as Mick said they were, was not at home. Mick gambled on Madge herself being too ashamed ever to reveal what had happened; if she did, he would laugh and say she was a silly kid who had imagined it all. After all, who would want to lay a hand on such an uninviting bit of goods?

Madge expected daily to hear that Widnes' Stores had been robbed. She could never tell Norman, nor anyone else, what had happened, even though she knew she should. Mick's assessment of her was shrewd; she felt totally degraded. Her whole body ached and on Friday she moved about like an old woman. Norman and Emma decided she must be having period pains; Norman treated her extra gently and felt that otherwise the most tactful thing was to pretend not to have noticed, though Emma thought he should send the girl home.

On Saturday Madge looked better; she had gone to bed early the night before, carrying on the pretence of a stomach upset. Her mother gave her bismuth and two aspirin, and she did in fact sleep, though she cried for ages first. In the morning the soreness was easier, and occasionally she was able to forget, just for a few minutes, what had happened.

She had also lost her new slacks, abandoned in their parcel behind the sports pavilion.

Mick was not going to rush it. He had to plan. It seemed that Emma was left alone at times, though not for long.

He spent Saturday afternoon with his friends tearing along the roads on their motor-bikes, cutting up the motorists. Later, they went to a pub.

"Not forgotten about that job, have you, Mick?" asked Terry as they lounged against the bar.

"Nah — got to set it up, haven't I?" Mick answered.

Terry had done some thieving, and Mick had been with him when they'd found a back door open in a Muddington side-street, just asking for them to step in and grab what they could. They'd nabbed a transistor radio, which Mick still used, and some cash. Terry had done a few other jobs; he'd been caught once, and put on probation. Mick, before he got the bike, had lifted an occasional car for the ride home and dumped it, but he had never been charged with anything. The challenge of getting something for nothing appealed to him; it was a shame to let an opportunity slip, and if someone was mug enough to leave stuff around for the taking, they deserved to lose it.

"Might be a good bit there," Terry said, in his experienced way. "Them small shops — ruddy gold mines. Like some help?"

But Mick thought not. He'd taken it on as a bet, hadn't he? Besides, now he'd got interested in the planning.

Reg, who had noticed a dark-haired bird across the bar and was trying to get her to look at him, did not hear this talk. He did not refer to Mick's rescue of Madge, either. He'd suffered plenty of ribbing in the past because his sister was so plain; trust her to go puking all over Muddington. It was decent of Mick to see to her, and too embarrassing to mention.

Late on the Saturday night Guy Curtis arrived back in Britain from South America. He had not told Paula he was coming, for he planned to go straight to his small London flat, but after he cleared customs he changed his mind. In just over an hour he could be in Bidbury: why not go, and see what sort of a welcome he got?

He collected his car from the long-stay garage where he had left it, and set off, arriving at half-past one in the morning.

The house was in darkness. He opened the back door, which was not locked, and went in through the kitchen. At once the Labrador got up and came over to him, wagging his tail and snorting with pleasure. There was no sign of the other dogs, though their empty feeding bowls were ranged across the floor. Guy patted Boris and walked into the hall. An odour of rather unsavoury stew clung to the house, and a smell of wet dog. He supposed the rest of the pack would hear him and start barking, but they might keep quiet if they recognized his tread. He went upstairs and looked into the room in which he expected to find Laura asleep. It was empty, and contained no cot. Guy continued on, and opened the main bedroom door.

He was not really surprised at what he found, and he did not stay to investigate.

As he went back through the house the four dogs who were in the dining-room began to bark. Guy could not know that they had been shut in there so that Harry could leave without them hurling themselves at his legs. They had never got used to him and would go for him if Paula was not there to call them off; jealous, she had said in her mocking way.

Guy got into his car and drove away. It was stupid to arrive in the middle of the night; Paula was not likely to change her habits. But things must be tidied up — he'd come some other time and have it out with her — see what she planned to do. He ought to find out how Laura was, he supposed.

He was dimly aware of a child's high cry above the barking of the dogs as he left, but it was not surprising that she had woken up with all the noise.

Being caught in the act was not in Harry's plans. It had never happened before. As soon as he heard the car drive off he leapt out of bed, flung on his clothes, and departed. To the astonishment of his family he spent all Sunday at home and as the weather was fine he worked in the garden, industriously planting broad beans and preparing the ground for other seeds.

Edna, as usual, did the washing. With going out to work all week she liked to get that done on Sunday. Madge helped her take it to the launderette round the corner in the plastic bags she kept for the purpose. The girl looked peaky; she hadn't got over her stomach upset yet — she'd scarcely touched her dinner.

Harry did not go out that evening. Edna knew the signs; he'd sickened of whatever woman he'd been running, or she of him, and would find his pleasure at home for a time. It wouldn't last, though. He'd be off again as soon as some fresh bit of skirt took his fancy.

But at least that doggy smell might leave him now.

Mrs Costello, that Sunday morning, was woken as usual by Pedro getting off the end of her bed and shuffling to the door, whining to go out. Without him she might easily sleep all morning. She let him into the garden, brought the paper in, and sat in her shabby dressing-gown at the kitchen table reading the gossipy bits and drinking four cups of instant coffee one after the other. Then she got ready for church, where she tried to imagine herself back in the past with Charles and the boys around her.

For lunch she warmed up the remains of a frozen shepherd's pie left from the day before. She had several glasses of sherry, too, and afterwards she slept. Then she took Pedro out. She'd meant to string cotton round the polyanthus to keep the birds off, but she didn't get round to it, although it was a fine afternoon. She had a new thriller from the library and started to read that when she returned from her walk, but she couldn't concentrate, so in the end she put the television on and spent the evening with that for company.

Because the weather was so fine, the Renshaws drove into the country that Sunday afternoon and went for a walk in the beech woods. The ground was drying out after the rain and it was soft and springy on the leaf-strewn paths through the trees. Jamie ran on ahead of his parents. The sunny afternoon had brought others out too, and there were a number of walkers in the woods, some with dogs. Jamie fell back and walked beside his parents after a red setter had pranced about in front of him waving its tail and inviting him to play. He put a hand on Claire's pushchair and said he would push her. It was hard work propelling it over the bumpy ground. As they came from one copse into a clearing they met the Armitages. Sarah was pushing Simon and Kenneth was throwing sticks for Gyp, who was over-excited and kept uttering sharp barks

The families went on together, and Kenneth began asking Lydia about the badminton club, which he thought of joining. It was a blow to learn that it met on the same night as the bellringers, but Lydia suggested that he might take up bridge instead. Unencumbered by either pushchair, they walked in front, while Sarah and Geoffrey, with the children, gradually fell behind. Gyp realized the games were over and calmed down; they met other dogs who came to investigate him, and he sniffed at them in return, but none were unduly hostile to him except a bull terrier which growled formidably. Gyp, no hero, bounded back in alarm, and as he did so Jamie looked thoroughly scared. Sarah noticed his grip tighten on Claire's chair, and he almost tipped her over.

She and Geoffrey at first communicated through the children, comparing their rates of growth and accomplishment, but then Sarah noticed some pussy willow, and Geoffrey pointed out wood anemones. Soon they were talking about wild flowers in general; Geoffrey had found edelweiss in the Alps, and Sarah dreamed of seeing asphodels in Greece. Lydia and Kenneth drew further and further ahead, and by the time they reached the cars, which were parked near one another, had been waiting for some time. They, too, had found plenty to talk about, and Lydia had invited the Armitages to dinner the following Thursday.

CHAPTER
TEN

Rose Hallam, out with her dachshunds, soon noticed Norman and Jamie together, and she quickly realized that their meetings were not accidental.

It seemed rather strange to her that they should walk down Funnel Lane every morning, and it was at the back of her mind when by chance she met Mrs Costello in New Bidbury one afternoon. Mrs Costello had toured the shopping centre looking out for the woman with the victimized child; she regarded it now as a duty to search for the pair. She had grown tired, and gone to the library for a rest, leaving Pedro tied up outside, for dogs were not admitted. Rose recognized him when she tethered the dachshunds while she popped in to see what books the library had about Sicily, where she and Bob were thinking of going for their holiday.

Mrs Costello had subsided on one of the rexine-covered benches, but when she saw Rose she got up and followed her out of the building. They untied their dogs and started up the road in company. Rose thought Mrs Costello looked exhausted and suggested that they should call in at The Honeypot for tea, where the proprietor knew that if she banned dogs she would lose a lot of custom, and admitted them as long as they were small and could be stowed away discreetly

Mrs Costello promptly devoured two toasted teacakes, some sandwiches and a large slice of cream cake, while Rose merely nibbled a biscuit. The poor old thing must be starving, Rose thought. She chatted away while Mrs Costello munched on, telling her about Marguerite's sale, the new spring fashions, and thus to trade in general, small shopkeepers in particular, and so to Widnes' Stores.

"Funny, isn't it," she said, "how Norman meets little Jamie Renshaw every day? They go down Funnel Lane. Have you noticed them? Jamie must be going to school. He shouldn't pass the square."

Mrs Costello had not seen them. She and Pedro did not go out until later.

"How odd," she said. "But then Norman leads a very peculiar sort of life."

Rose agreed that it could not be easy.

"I never knew why he married her," said Mrs Costello. "I've always thought she must have some sort of hold over him."

Rose laughed. "She was attractive, in a blowsy sort of way, I remember," she said. "The age difference probably didn't matter then. After all, a younger wife could have had an accident and ended up an invalid too. It happens."

"I didn't mean that sort of hold," said Mrs Costello, stirring her third cup of tea. She was feeling better now after her intake of carbohydrate. "I was thinking that she might know something about him he wouldn't want spread around." She sipped her tea while Rose looked perplexed. "His mother died very suddenly in the end, didn't she?"

Rose did not understand the inference at first.

"People do die suddenly," she said at last, startled and shocked.

"That's as may be," said Mrs Costello. "The house would have been full of powerful drugs. It would have been easy enough."

Although Rose had been the one to raise the subject of Norman's conduct, she thought this was going too far and headed Mrs Costello off the subject by offering her another cake. That night, though, she told Bob.

"Hm. Poor old Mrs C. must be going a bit gaga, starting that sort of of rumour," he said. "Though I suppose it's not altogether so fanciful. How does one know what one would do in such a situation, after all? Mrs Widnes might have asked Norman to give her an overdose."

"All the more reason to keep quiet, if she did," said Rose. "But surely Emma wouldn't have blackmailed him into marrying her, would she?"

"You've only to read the newspapers to see that stranger things happen every day," said Bob.

Whenever she got the chance, Madge took to peering inside Emma's wardrobe to make sure the safe was still there. She made little excuses to go to the bedroom to fetch a library book, a clean handkerchief, or Emma's solid cologne stick with which she wiped brow and wrists throughout the day. She had an idea that Mick might manage to steal it without the theft being noticed for several days, but it was a silly thought really for Norman put the takings in it every evening when he cashed up and it would be missed at once, even if Mick left no other sign of his visit. Each time Madge looked, she would touch it as if it were some sort of talisman.

"Madge is very restless," Emma remarked after some days of this. "She used to like sitting here chatting, but now she's for ever bobbing about looking for errands. I believe she's losing weight, too."

It was true. Madge had not entirely stopped eating, but the craving she shared with Emma for rich, sweet things had gone, and she only pecked at the meals her mother provided.

Sarah had to miss her yoga class because it was the only night possible for the Renshaws' dinner party. Naturally hers were the arrangements that had to be scrapped: nothing could be allowed to interfere with Kenneth's commitments. What with them, and Lydia's bridge, badminton and upholstery, it was quite tricky to fit it in at all. Simon was to go too, to save a baby-sitter; Sarah, in any case, was not organized for finding one.

"You must ask Lydia about it," Kenneth instructed. "I'm sure she never needs to refuse an invitation for want of one."

Sarah nearly retorted that as they never went out together they had hitherto not felt this lack, but it was not worth the effort. She looked at him as he walked about their bedroom buttoning up his clean shirt, and thought how ridiculous he seemed, with his pale legs exposed under its lavender hem.

When they arrived at the Renshaws, Simon, in the carry-cot which he had now outgrown, was put on the floor in Claire's room. He would not be safe on a bed, for if he woke and sat up he might topple the whole thing over. He was sleepy, and lay there placidly enough.

Jamie was still awake; his bedroom door was open and Sarah could see him sitting up in bed, reading. She looked in to say good night before going downstairs to join the others.

His wallpaper was crimson, with jungle animals striding about all over it. Maroon curtains printed with bears hung across his window.

Sarah was startled by all this vivid display.

"Good gracious, Jamie, are you going to be a lion-tamer when you grow up?" she asked.

"Mum chose it," said Jamie. "I wanted ships, but she said animals are living." He looked at the wall beside him with distaste. "I don't like them," he confided. "They look real."

In the dim light from his bedside lamp, they did. Sarah imagined how they might seem to swell and move if he let his mind dwell on them.

"They're only pictures," she said. "Nothing to worry about."

"I know. But telling yourself things doesn't always cure you," Jamie said.

Sarah found it sad that he should have discovered this truth so early in life.

"It helps," she told him.

Geoffrey put a large drink into her hand when she came into the sitting-room, and then the Hallams arrived.

Lydia had decided that while she was about it, she would make it a real party. She wanted to cultivate the Hallams who could be useful friends; she had first met Rose at a charity coffee morning, and if she could ever persuade Geoffrey to take up golf, such a socially helpful hobby, Bob Hallam could be the means of getting him into the club.

Kenneth was delighted when he saw the other guests; his worry now was that Sarah might let him down. He saw, with disapproval, that she was accepting a second drink from Geoffrey, who had made some sort of cocktail; it tasted innocent, but Kenneth knew already that it was not, after only half a glass. How foolish: surely there would be wine with dinner? Sherry was the proper drink to offer. His opinion of Geoffrey took a downward turn.

Sarah suddenly began to sparkle. At dinner she found that Rose was interested in yoga, so they talked about that. Then Geoffrey, when he had finished carving the capon, remembered that they had discussed flowers before, and revived that subject. Sarah held forth knowledgeably; she had planned to read biology at university, but marriage to Kenneth had changed all that. Bob said she should read for a degree at home; she might enrol with the Open University. Everyone except Kenneth thought it a splendid idea, and Sarah pretended that she might actually do it, though she knew she would never make the effort.

Through all this talk, Kenneth wore a boot-faced look; the conversation kept excluding him, and he made several efforts to get into it, only succeeding when he mentioned bellringing. But even then Sarah took attention from him by complaining that Simon had not been able to get to sleep the evening before because of the weekly practice.

"You should hear Kitty Minter about the bells," said Rose. "One of these Wednesdays you'll find she's been up the tower and cut the ropes. She hates them. It's all the overtones, of course."

"What do you mean?" asked Lydia.

"The echoes. The sound reverberates — it's like when you hold the pedal down on a piano and sustain several notes in discord," said Rose. "Some people are very susceptible to it — others don't notice. That's why people are so sharply divided about bellringing."

"You ringers don't hear them properly yourselves, when you're up the tower," Bob pointed out.

"People can be killed by the noise," said Sarah, who had read *The Nine Tailors*.

"It's a pleasant sound heard from a distance, but I don't think I'd like it if I lived next to the church," said Bob.

He thought it a selfish hobby, since it was practised by only eight or so people and afflicted discomfort upon many involuntary listeners, but he did not want to wreck the Renshaws' party by antagonizing a fellow guest, so he kept this opinion to himself.

"Likes and dislikes are funny things, aren't they?" said Sarah, too animated by her sudden social success to be discreet. "Animals, for instance. Some people don't like them."

She had intended to mention Jamie's wallpaper, but she lost her chance. Bob seized the opportunity to lead the conversation away from the controversial bells.

"That's another of Kitty's hates," he said. "I do like Kitty — she's so direct — never hesitates to say what she thinks, however unpopular her view. She says there are far too many dogs in Bidbury."

"There are too many big dogs, that's certain," Geoffrey said. "It's one thing in the country — but it isn't fair to keep big dogs in urban areas."

Sarah wondered if Gyp qualified as large.

"Jamie doesn't like dogs, does he?" she said.

At this both Lydia and Geoffrey looked startled.

"Why do you say that, Sarah?" Geoffrey asked her.

"Didn't you notice on Sunday, when Gyp ran towards him from that bull terrier? He looked quite scared," Sarah said. "And he knows Gyp — he shouldn't be afraid of him."

Rose, busy dissecting a wing of the capon, did not see the horrified glance which Lydia and Geoffrey exchanged at this disclosure.

"Why does Jamie meet Norman Widnes on his way to school every morning?" she asked. "I've noticed them in the square. Norman takes him to school, I suppose."

"What do you mean, Rose? Jamie doesn't go through the square to get to school. He goes along Foster Avenue. It must be some other child," said Lydia.

But Rose knew Jamie.

"It's Jamie all right," she said. "And he comes into the square every morning at a quarter to nine."

"He isn't late for school," said Lydia, still disbelieving. "Or if he is, we haven't been told."

"I expect Norman just likes a stroll before he opens the shops," said Rose, but she had clearly unnerved her host and hostess by her remark.

After this the evening was less successful and the conversation often faltered. When they got home, Rose said that in spite of the shock her disclosure had been, she was glad that Geoffrey and Lydia now knew, and Bob agreed.

"After all, if anything was wrong and I hadn't told them, I'd feel terrible," she argued.

"I'm convinced, dear," Bob said. "But it's not very likely that Norman would meet him openly, if it was."

"Nothing may have happened yet," said Rose. "He may be preparing the way."

Kenneth, removing his lavender shirt, accused Sarah of drinking too much and losing her self-control. He reproved her for fifteen minutes. Sarah knew he was right, but it was Jamie, not herself or Kenneth, whom she had betrayed.

CHAPTER
ELEVEN

"Don't say a word to him," warned Geoffrey, the next morning.

As they cleared up after the party, he and Lydia had grimly discussed what there could be between Jamie and Norman. Geoffrey's main concern was with the character of his son: the boy had been revealed as afraid of dogs; he might easily be weak in other ways too.

For once Lydia's placidity deserted her. No child of hers could be permitted fear of animals and he must be cured forthwith, but she thought Jamie too young to have developed the other sort of tendency. Conceding this, Geoffrey pointed out that he was not too young to be debased.

Jamie left for school with fair eagerness, and now that Lydia thought about it, this was a recent development. Breakfast had been rather a silent affair until Claire livened it up by depositing some of her cereal on the floor and Jamie had then tried wondering aloud whether, if he saved and saved, he might manage to buy a bicycle.

"We'll see about that," said Geoffrey curtly into the *Guardian*.

When he departed, Jamie followed by his father who wore an old raincoat and cap. Lydia at once grabbed Claire and rushed round next door to Sarah.

"Geoff's following Jamie to see what he and Norman Widnes get up to every morning," she gasped. "He's gone off in a sleazy old mac like that private eye on television. Here, take Claire. I'm going to see what happens."

And before Sarah could speak she had rushed from the house. Sarah, through the window, saw her back the car out of the drive and set off up the road.

When Jamie turned up Funnel Lane, Geoffrey loitered in a gateway at the end of it. Just as Rose had said, after a while he reappeared with Norman. The two seemed to be talking earnestly with Jamie hopping along, waving his arms about as he spoke. Geoffrey seldom saw his son so animated at home, and he felt a physical ache at the sight which he was honest enough, even in his anxious state, to recognize as jealousy.

He hid behind some laurel bushes, hoping the householder would not emerge to flush him out. Jamie and Norman went past and turned up Lincoln Road. Geoffrey fell in behind. There wasn't much time for anything to happen if the child was to be punctual at school; but there was that empty house on the way, with the overgrown garden offering cover enough for all sorts of activity. If Jamie were five minutes late probably no one would mind very much.

As the two ahead turned into Foster Avenue, Geoffrey saw Norman take the little boy's hand. He broke into a trot to pursue them faster, closing the gap as he rounded the corner himself. They were walking along sedately, hand in hand. Geoffrey did not notice the dog until Norman and Jamie stepped into the road to avoid it; then, after another few yards, Jamie let go of Norman's hand and ran on, without a backward glance.

Norman began walking back the way he had come, and when he reached the corner found a very angry man waiting for him.

"You meet my son every morning," Geoffrey accused. He tried to be calm; on the evidence of this morning it was unlikely that anything had happened — yet.

Norman's sole instinct was to defend Jamie from possible charges of cowardice.

"That's right," he said genially. "It takes but a few minutes of my time."

"Why?" thundered Geoffrey. "You have no right to do it. I forbid you to speak to the boy again."

Norman, bewildered, stared at the other man. It had taken him a moment to absorb the fact that here was Jamie's father; it took more before he understood what was now implied, and when he did, he took a deep breath in an effort to control his own immediate fury.

"Mr Renshaw, your lad is scared of that Alsatian dog, which stands in the way every morning," he said. "It seems gentle enough, granted; but the boy was coming round by the square every morning to avoid it, and being late for school."

"That's a neat excuse," said Geoffrey, seething.

"It's the reason," said Norman.

"Why didn't you come and tell me, then, instead of meeting him?

"Because he thought you might be angry — and he was right, you are," said Norman, who had discussed this course with Jamie only the day before.

"How long has this been going on?" Geoffrey demanded."

"About a week," said Norman. "I hoped he'd get over it, given time. And I've asked Mrs Curtis to keep her dog in, but it's made no difference. Perhaps she'll listen to you, if you ask her. Now, if you'll excuse me, I must get back to my shop," and he swept past Geoffrey and stalked on up the road.

A moment later Lydia, in the car, drew up beside Geoffrey.

"Well?" she said, as he got into the car. She had parked near the school and watched Jamie arrive.

"He's afraid of that dog — up there — the Alsatian. So Widnes said," Geoffrey told her. "What an excuse."

He went off late to his office unable to decide which of the reasons he preferred to accept.

It was no good trying to protect Jamie now, Sarah knew. His secret was out, and she was basely relieved that Rose had shared her responsibility for its disclosure.

"It's not so awful. He'll grow out of it," she said, when Lydia related what had happened.

"Geoff thinks there's more to it, on Norman Widnes' part," said Lydia.

Sarah felt wise, a most unusual sensation for her.

"Norman Widnes is all right," she stated.

"Well — why didn't he come and tell us about it?"

"Who? Jamie? Children often don't tell their parents things," said Sarah.

"No — Norman Widnes. Geoff would have taken Jamie by car again," said Lydia. But would he? He might have said that Jamie must conquer his fear. "Or I'd have gone with him," she added.

"Would you?" asked Sarah.

"Of course — you'd have Claire for a few minutes, wouldn't you, while I popped along? It takes such ages bundling her into her outdoor clothes," said Lydia, rubbing her forehead.

"Would you like an aspirin?" asked Sarah. She could not get over seeing Lydia brought so low.

"No — I'm all right. Thanks, though, Sarah." Lydia made an effort. "Well, I suppose we must decide what to do."

"What did Geoffrey say to Norman?"

"Minced him up properly, I think," said Lydia.

"He'll have to accept what Norman said, surely," Sarah said. Geoffrey liked wild flowers and Mahler: he must be capable of understanding a sensitive little boy. It was not as if he were like Kenneth.

"I'll get a dog. I'll get one today," Lydia decided, reviving at the thought of some positive action. "You must come with me, Sarah. We'll go into town."

"You can't get one just like that," Sarah protested, dismayed at such an impulsive plan. "You must talk to Geoff about it. Didn't you say you were going to wait until you move to the country?"

"That's Geoff's idea. He thinks we need more space. But you manage Gyp all right."

Sarah found time to note that this was the first commendation she had ever received from Lydia.

"I get a bit worn out," she confessed. "I feel he must have a walk every day, whether I want one or not. Sometimes when it's pouring with rain I hate it. And pushing the pram with him on a lead is hard work — he often heads off in a different direction to where you want to go."

"We needn't have such a big dog. A spaniel, perhaps, or some sort of terrier," said Lydia. "It must be Jamie's responsibility to look after it. Animals exist on another level of consciousness from ours, and he must learn to relate to it."

She was recovering, Sarah saw.

"If you got a small puppy, perhaps he'd get used to it as it grows," she said slowly. "But there's the training, and everything." It seemed to her very wrong to impose the task and duties of dog ownership on a reluctant child. "I'm not keen on Alsatians myself — and if you're as small as Jamie they must look pretty alarming," she said. "Even Gyp's big enough to knock him over by leaning against him, without meaning any harm."

"I'll ring Geoff and see if he thinks I should get a puppy this afternoon," said Lydia, as if Sarah had not spoken.

It was unlike her to voice indecision at any time.

"I should leave it for now," Sarah advised. "There's the weekend ahead — think about it. If you do get one, you must go into it carefully. You can't rush into having just any old puppy."

This was good counsel, and Lydia went off, with Claire tucked under her arm, saying she would ponder well. Sarah was left feeling stimulated by the excitement and her own unusual role as sage. She wondered how Norman felt about Geoffrey's insinuations.

He ought to be very angry.

He was. He came into the shop with a set face and stumped out to the store without a word to Madge or a customer who was buying a torch, and he could be heard out there noisily shifting boxes about for ten minutes. Then he went upstairs to Emma. She had seen him striding across the square with his fists clenched by his sides and a furious look on his face.

That black look frightened her. In spite of all that had happened, she had never seen it before.

That afternoon Lydia met Jamie at school. They did not refer to the morning's events, but they walked down Foster Avenue and when they drew near the gate where the Alsatian usually stood, Jamie took hold of the handle of Claire's pushchair and began to look anxious.

The dog was not in sight, but as they passed the gateway he came bounding out, huge tail waving, tongue bared as he barked at them, several short, sharp sounds, deep in his throat, and Jamie quailed.

"He won't hurt you," Lydia said firmly, facing facts but she was not so foolish as to recommend patting a strange dog. "It's like wasps," she explained as they went on, the dog now stationary, watching them. "They don't hurt you if you leave them alone. You must learn to understand all living things and make them your friends."

Understanding wasps was not easy, Jamie knew, nor were they friendly. One had stung him severely only last September.

Mick Green had seen a smart leather coat with a fur collar that he fancied. He was tired of his studded jacket; there was no class to it, and besides, it was tight across his shoulders, for he had filled out since he bought it. But he couldn't lash out on the coat right away; it cost over sixty pounds. If he wanted it quick, and he did, he'd have to get hold of some cash.

CHAPTER
TWELVE

Once a week Dr Barrett came to see Emma. On Friday afternoon he called, and told Norman that her blood pressure was up.

"She must lose some weight," he said.

Norman did not see how this could be done.

"I watch her diet very strictly," he said.

The doctor believed him, but was sure that Emma somehow got hold of contraband food, and he could not altogether blame her. It was his duty, however, to issue a warning.

"Well — you understand the position," he said.

Later, Norman spoke to Madge.

"If Mrs Widnes wants you to buy chocolates for her, Madge, you mustn't," he said. "It may seem unkind to you, but the doctor says she's too heavy and it puts a strain on her heart."

Madge blushed guiltily and bent her head over the tray of scouring pads she had been tidying. She had never bought anything for Emma, though; she had merely given her what Mrs Bowling had already hidden.

Just before closing time, Mick Green entered the shop.

Madge's heart gave a lurch when she saw him saunter in, hands in pockets, leather jacket undone to display a grinning wolf mask on the chest of his purple singlet. He behaved as if they had never met. After inspecting some pocket knives arranged on a revolving stand, he chose one and was served by Norman. Whistling, waiting for his change, he peered past the counter to the lobby beyond, where on the right, as Madge had told him, the stairs ascended to the flat above. Up there, in a small steel safe, the weekend takings would be placed.

Madge felt rather sick when he had gone, and was glad that it would soon be time to go home.

"What upset you this morning?" Emma at last asked Norman.

The shop was closed, the curtains were drawn in the flat, the television was on, and Norman was sitting at the table making up the books.

In the end, he told her about Geoffrey Renshaw's imputation.

"Is that all?" Emma was relieved. "Well — send him up to me, that Mr Renshaw," she said and laughed, the huge coarse laugh which made her whole frame vibrate. "There's nothing like that about you, and I should know."

Once, Norman had loved to hear her cheerful laughter; now, he had to hide a shudder. He went on totting up figures.

"What are you going to do?" Emma asked. "You won't take the boy again, will you?"

"I haven't thought about it," Norman said. His brain felt overloaded with all its problems: Emma; Felicity; and at the moment, Value Added Tax. Jamie was another on the list.

"Poor little lad," said Emma genially. "It seems a shame."

His parents did not mention the subject to Jamie, but when he was in bed that night they talked of nothing else. Lydia said that in future she would take him to school, and walk him past the dog until familiarity cured him.

"He must conquer this," Geoffrey said. "He really must."

They decided to buy him a dog for his birthday next month, and in the meantime promote in him a state of wanting one.

"He really wants a bike," Lydia said. "But that will have to wait."

"The roads are far too dangerous," said Geoffrey.

Pedro, snuffling about in the garden among the early crocus on Saturday morning, heard a voice calling to him softly from the roadway.

"Good dog, then. Come along, boy," it said, and Pedro smelled a familiar meaty odour.

Investigating, he found the gate to the road open, and an enticing scent beckoning him out. A little trail of Meatimix, sprinkled on the ground, led from the gate to the pavement, and he shuffled along, licking up the morsels as he went.

"Good boy," said Mick, as he emerged. No one was in sight, and in seconds he had gathered up the heavy dog and bundled him into the back of a small green van he had borrowed without its owner's permission from a

104

street in New Bidbury earlier that morning. He drove off with the dog, towards the country.

Pedro had not barked once.

That same Saturday Kenneth Armitage went out for the day with the bellringers. They were visiting a church on the other side of the county to ring the fine set of bells in its tower. When he had gone, Sarah relaxed. She had plenty of time to prepare for Sunday so that it might pass without discord; she could catch up on the ironing; she might even read a novel. But first she had a mission: Kenneth had instructed her to call at Widnes Store and buy some rawlplugs, for he wanted to put up some shelves in the small bedroom he used as a study over the weekend. He was good at doing odd jobs about the place and spent much of his spare time on home improvements.

Sarah knew that she might easily forget this errand if she did not do it at once, so she set out in the morning. As she came into the square she met Mrs Costello, who looked distraught.

"Oh Sarah, have you seen Pedro anywhere? He's disappeared," the old lady said.

Sarah hadn't. She was shocked by Mrs Costello's appearance: her face was pinched and blue; her wild hair more unruly even than usual; and she wore no coat, so that the keen wind cut at her thin body which was wrapped in a long, shapeless cardigan.

"I've looked everywhere," said Mrs Costello. "There isn't a sign of him."

"You'll catch cold, Mrs Costello. Do go home and get a coat at least," Sarah said. "Have you looked thoroughly

105

in the house? Perhaps he's got locked into a cupboard or something."

The dog was old; he wouldn't stray far, Sarah thought. He might have collapsed somewhere in the house or garden — and his mistress would soon collapse too, she feared.

In the end, Sarah persuaded Mrs Costello to turn back to her own cottage, which she had left unlocked. Sarah parked Simon's pushchair in the hall and tied Gyp to the banister rail, then went with the old lady all over the house and garden, but saw no sign of Pedro. The gate into Lincoln Road was closed, and she did not notice a small trace of Meatimix on the ground near it.

"He sleeps on my bed," said Mrs Costello, taking Sarah into her room, where there was a smell of elderly dog and grubby garments.

"Mrs Costello, do come and sit down and let me make you some tea," begged Sarah. "Then we'll decide what to do."

She felt that really they ought to call the doctor, but tea, to begin with, might help. Mrs Costello began to cry when they were in the kitchen, and Sarah hunted about until she found some brandy in a cupboard among a heap of empty gin bottles. She poured what was left in the bottle into a glass and gave it to Mrs Costello, who looked better after she had swallowed it.

It was, however, a great relief when Mrs Minter walked in through the front door and took brisk command.

Mick, watching the area, had seen Mrs Costello out walking with the dog and had realized that he was not

106

fierce; it was his warning barks that made him a threat. If dumped, he might find his way home, so some distance from Bidbury Mick stopped his van and dragged Pedro by the collar into a field. The dog made no attempt to escape, although he was bewildered at being tugged along in so unmannerly a way; he tried to ingratiate himself by licking his captor's hand.

Mick had no trouble in finding a stone large enough to smash the dog's thin skull at a blow.

He abandoned the van in Muddington, and thumbed a lift back to New Bidbury where he lived with his parents in a block of council flats.

His motor-bike had stayed at home throughout the operation.

Lydia said, "How would you like to go to the safari park tomorrow, Jamie?" There was one about thirty miles away. "Wouldn't it be fun?"

Geoffrey stared at her. She had not mentioned this idea to him. They were having lunch in the kitchen. Claire sat in her high chair waving a spoon around and occasionally stirring her porridge-like mess of minced meat and vegetables; Jamie, until now, had been enjoying his baked potato and fresh salad with cottage cheese, although he would have preferred sausage and chips.

"Would we have to get out of the car?" he asked cautiously.

"You'd want to, to see the animals better."

Jamie was silent. He imagined himself having to stand amid a pack of hungry lions, and his mother did not think of explaining that the public were not allowed to get out of their cars where the animals were dangerous.

"Man and the animal kingdom have special links," she said. "You must start to understand about them."

Geoffrey's spirits, already low, sank further still. If only she could be less intense about all this.

"Years and years ago," Lydia went on, in a *Listen With Mother* voice, "man provoked the animals to become attackers. There's an African legend which tells that man and the animals used to live as friends till the gods sent man the gift of fire, and then the animals fled."

"Fire came when the iron age men struck flints," said Jamie, earning his father's silent admiration.

"I said it was a legend. Lots of legends have some truth in them," Lydia said patiently. "Well — we'll go, then, unless it's a very wet day."

"Wouldn't it be better to wait a month or two, till the weather's more settled?" Geoffrey suggested. He had brought a complex report home from the office and planned to study it in peace over the weekend.

"It will be more crowded then," said Lydia.

Geoffrey, helping himself to more grated carrot, gave up.

Father and son, at bedtime, both prayed for rain.

Mick had learned from Madge that the back door of Widnes' Stores, beyond the lobby, was glass-paned, and led into the small garden which ran alongside the greengrocer's. That, in turn, was next to Mrs Costello's. Two men lived above the greengrocer's, Madge had said, but they kept no pets and were seldom seen around.

The greengrocer lived in New Bidbury. The rooms over Bodger's Self-Service were used for stock. Mr Bodger had a house in Wilberforce Road.

Mick had thought about forcing Madge to steal a key or get an impression in soap from one, but had given up that idea; he had already taken her to the limit. She had admitted that Norman sometimes left Emma alone for short periods, and every Saturday night went down to The Grapes. Emma had told her so.

On Saturday evening Mick rode his motor-bike into the square and stopped opposite the shop, revving the engine and staring about him. Two girls were in the bus shelter, and he aimed a few remarks at them, though the force of what he said was wasted because of the noise from the bike's exhaust. Nostrils flaring, like a wicked knight on a snorting palfrey, he roared off and circled round to Lincoln Road at the back of the shops. His plan was not complete in all its details; if he left the bike in the road someone might notice and remember it after the robbery; it might even get nicked. He had seen an empty house somewhere nearby that morning when he came in the van and took the dog. At the time he'd noticed it as a possible hide-out. He cut the engine and wheeled the bike up its driveway, where he hid it among the bushes. He'd time for a smoke before going into action.

Mrs Costello refused to have supper with Mrs Minter that evening, for Pedro might come home and it would be dreadful if he couldn't get in. She propped the garden gate open a little way, and she left the back door ajar, just in case she did not hear him.

"Will you be all right if I slip out for an hour or so, dear?" asked Norman, as he always did on a Saturday.

Their evening meal had been steamed plaice with tomatoes and greens, followed by fresh young rhubarb gently stewed with sweetener instead of sugar. Norman still felt hungry, and so did Emma, but there was a large slice of Dundee cake in the drawer of her bedside table and as soon as Norman had gone she could eat it without fear of discovery.

"There's a good film on television," she said. "I'll be happy enough with that."

Norman got her to bed before he left, putting the portable colour television set close enough for her to reach the controls, and arranging the telephone beside her, in case of emergency.

He did go to The Grapes; he always did when he said he would, in case she telephoned. Though they would tell her he had left, her trust in him would remain; she would think he had gone for a walk. Norman refused to accept Felicity's theory that Emma knew about them.

She had never yet needed to ring The Grapes.

CHAPTER
THIRTEEN

Mick was surprised to find Mrs Costello's garden gate unlatched. He was sure he had closed it properly after abducting the dog. All was quiet, but a light burned at a downstairs window. Mick went silently up the path and approached the house, drawn by the orange oblong to peer in from the shelter of a large shrub which grew close by.

He could see the old woman dozing by the fire; her thin, knobbled legs, in woollen stockings, were thrust before her, and her feet, in worn felt bedroom slippers, rested on a low stool. Mouth open, she looked as if she might be dead. The room was full of heavy furniture which to Mick's eye looked hideous; there were some china objects about the place, but he saw no glint of silver, so he decided not to pay Mrs Costello a personal visit. When he noticed the back door propped open against a brick he hesitated, but only for a few seconds: he had come to do Widnes' Stores, where he was sure of several hundred pounds. Best stick to that and not lumber himself with stuff that might be hard to sell and anyway could be traced.

By means of the coal bin he was able to slide over the wall and into the greengrocer's garden. There was a light on in the flat above the shop, and Mick could hear music. It wasn't pop: more like that Radio Three stuff; but it should mask any noise he might make below.

It was more difficult to find a way over the next fence, which was an interwoven one. Mick worked his way along it, testing it, and then, finding a hurdle that seemed less firm than the rest, decided that a good shove might bring it down.

In fact, it took several attempts before the fence gave with a splintering crash which seemed to Mick as loud as a thunderclap overhead. He paused, motionless, but nothing happened.

At that moment Norman was settling Emma with the television, and the loud title music which heralded the film drowned the noise in the garden.

When nothing happened, Mick moved forward into Norman's plot. He was in dead trouble now if anyone came out of the shop, but he was bigger than that Widnes: a kick where it hurt most, and then the boot — that would do it. He'd be ready, too, expecting trouble; the others wouldn't.

He moved closer to the building, until he could see the glass-paned back door which Madge had described. Beside it was the store, built on to the original structure but entered from within, through the lobby which he had seen from the shop that morning.

After a while the light came on in the lobby and Mick saw a figure moving to and fro. If Norman were going out, he had to leave by the shop entrance for there was no other way into the street, but all the same it was a relief when the light went out. That meant he'd either returned upstairs, or left the place, closing the door from the lobby into the shop behind him.

Madge had sworn that there wasn't a burglar alarm; but even if there were, Mick could be away across the gardens before anyone saw him.

He went up to the back door and with his gloved fist knocked out the glass in one of the panes. He put his hand inside and turned the key. The door still did not yield, so it must be bolted. Mick had foreseen this, and had brought a hacksaw with him. He had bought it in New Bidbury, that morning before nicking the van — not at Widnes' Stores, where its purchase might be remembered. It didn't take him long to saw through several of the struts supporting the rest of the glass, which soon shattered, until there was a hole big enough for him to climb through. He made quite a lot of noise, but no one noticed.

While she watched the Saturday film, Mrs Minter cleaned the silver. She felt guilty when she sat idly; now indulging herself by watching an old film which starred James Mason, she was not entirely wasting her time.

The Hallams were coming to lunch the next day, and she must persuade Jane Costello to come too; she was bereft by the loss of Pedro and would hardly be cheerful company, but perhaps the dog would have turned up by then.

The film was interrupted at a poignant moment by the commercial, and for some seconds bowls of glutinous-looking Meatimix were drooled over by a small girl with a Yorkshire terrier clasped in her arm. Both dog and child slavered. How nauseous, thought Mrs Minter, polishing hard at a Georgian coffee-pot. Then she rebuked herself; she had grown too intolerant; her disapproval of the current dog cult was, perhaps, because she had rejected all love herself. But, she reflected, she had not rejected human love: it had rejected her, for Hugh had been killed and her son Derek, whom she had brought up to be independent, was in Canada, so she had to manage alone. To use an animal as a *raison d'être* was not her way.

But Jane Costello was different, and to be pitied. She needed Pedro, and apart from his constant yapping he was, Mrs Minter had to admit, an amiable dog.

There was now a cat on the screen lapping up Pussipi. Mrs Minter thought of the tons of protein consumed by domestic pets all over the globe and then of the starving humans: it didn't make sense. To take her mind off it, she got up then and there to telephone Jane Costello about tomorrow's lunch.

The telephone rang and rang in Mrs Costello's house, but there was no reply. Perhaps she had gone out again, wandering about looking for Pedro. Mrs Minter sighed. If there was still no answer later she would go across.

The commercials had ended, and Mrs Minter returned to her television. Her acquaintances who thought her so down to earth would have been surprised if they could have seen the dreamy pleasure with which she watched James Mason, an actor she had always admired, performing in a romantic costume drama.

Norman was in and out of The Grapes in ten minutes. He drank half a pint of bitter and bought a bottle of wine; his weekly routine. As he hurried down the path beside Mrs Minter's house he sucked a peppermint. It was not nice for Felicity if he arrived reeking of beer. How sordid it was, he thought as he hurried along: the secrecy; the haste. There was never enough time — never time to talk, never a whole night, and all because so long ago he had been obsessed by Emma.

He remembered the doctor's warning. Too often now he found himself thinking that she might not live much longer.

According to Madge, Emma watched television every night, so Mick should be able to get into the bedroom without being heard. The safe was portable; he could carry it down and break it open in the garden. He went upstairs softly, his gloved hand stretched before him to feel the way.

At the top, light filtered out on to the landing from a half-open door on the right, and he could hear voices coming from the television. James Mason, at present delighting Mrs Minter, had been giving Emma much the same nostalgic pleasure.

Surely Madge had said that the living-room, where Emma would be, was on the left? The bedroom, his goal, was on the right. She must have got it wrong, the silly bitch — couldn't tell right from left.

Mick tried the door on the left. It was securely closed, but it opened without a sound as he turned the knob and gently pushed. He had brought a pocket torch, and he shone it round.

It was the living-room. Madge had not been wrong. But it was empty. Mick looked quickly through the cupboards and found Mrs Bowling's housekeeping purse in a drawer. There was a five-pound note and some loose change in it, which he took.

Then he went on to the landing and peered through the crack of the open door. He had to get in there to find the safe. He had never imagined that Emma might be in bed, and mentally he cursed Madge for not telling him. It was hardly likely that he would be able to creep in under cover of the sound from the television and help himself, but he was not going to be put off now: the woman was helpless, after all.

Cautiously, he pushed the door a little wider, and saw Emma.

He had a shock. She was a hideous sight: a great white bloated face and reddened lips. One of her more courageous endeavours was the daily task of painting on a facial mask to keep herself pretty, as she put it, for Norman, and she had not yet removed it, though cream and tissues were beside her. She wore a lacy-knit bedjacket which had fallen apart over her huge breasts; they lay half exposed, like great sagging melons, but even in the dim light cast by one lamp and the reflected colours from the television screen, ivory white. Mick stared at her, repelled.

She seemed to be heavily asleep. High on drugs, most likely; she was sick, wasn't she?

Purposely, Mick made a small sound, knocking against the wall with his foot. Emma did not stir.

He'd be able to get in and out without her noticing. He knew just where to find the safe.

He crossed to the wardrobe, opened it, and as the door squeaked slightly turned to look at the woman in the bed, but she never moved. The big metal box was just where Madge had told him it would be, on the floor, beyond several pairs of shoes. He lifted it, but though it was heavy it could be carried. He'd never be able to open it without some sort of tool, but there would be plenty of them below, in the shop or the store.

Mick pulled the safe out, careless now in his excitement, and he scraped it against the side of the wardrobe. Just then, Emma woke, and Mick, with the safe held to his chest, saw her gazing at him with small, pig-like eyes sunk in the fleshy folds of her face. She opened her mouth and a weird groaning sound emerged.

Mick did not pause to remind himself that she was completely helpless. He acted on impulse, and repeated what he had done earlier to Pedro, for he already held the weapon.

In fact, Emma died from a gigantic coronary attack brought on by shock, seconds before he crashed the safe down on her head.

CHAPTER
FOURTEEN

Wide awake in bed, Jamie worried about the morrow. From his wallpaper and curtains the jungle beasts gazed down upon him, and he imagined their eyes, shining bright, boring into him, seeking the tastiest bits to devour. He had heard other children describe tigers brushing against their car, and apes playing with the radio aerials. Suppose his mother made him touch an ape?

He got out of bed and looked out of the window at the night sky. Would it rain? There were no clouds; he could see a sliver of moon and some distant stars. Below, the french window opened and his parents came out on to the small paved patio. Their voices floated up to him.

"He'll be thrilled to have a dog of his own," said his mother. "It will be the best birthday present we could give him. He must look after it himself right from the beginning — take it out before he goes to school, feed it, and so on."

They moved away before his father answered, the sound of their voices fading, and Jamie leaned against the window sill feeling rather sick. A dog of his own! How would he bear it?

He remembered some puppies that had belonged to a friend of his — or rather, the mother dog had. Then these puppies had been born. But their eyes were shut and they were bald-looking. He didn't like them much. Next time he saw them he'd been given one to hold. Its racing little heart had alarmed him, thudding against his hand, and its pink, distended belly had quivered disturbingly. Then it had peed all down his sweater and he hadn't thought it a joke, as his friend had done.

He got back into bed and lay panicking. How could he tell his parents that he didn't want a dog? It would cost a lot — as much as a bike, probably. If it was his, perhaps he could sell it. He could give the money back to his parents. But it was ungrateful to sell a present. Perhaps he could give it to a blind man; his parents wouldn't make a blind man give it back.

Jamie's mind raced round in a ferment while his well-intentioned parents, all unknowing, planned to take him close to breaking-point.

In the distance Jamie heard a motor-bike racing down some local road, but he paid it no attention. His mind was on his own small, tormented universe.

Felicity put a Mozart Piano Concerto on the record player and tried not to look at the time. What sort of life was this, coming back to a solitary room and spending her Saturday nights, waiting for the hurried visits of someone else's husband?

She thought of the sweeping mountain ranges of the Canadian Rockies. Out there she might find someone prepared to devote at least a good part of his life to her.

She started a letter to the headmaster of a school in British Columbia, but had got no further than the first paragraph when she heard Norman's key in the door. As always, despite her intellectual efforts at resistance, a surge of pleasure filled her. He had managed to get away; she was not alone; he needed her.

"Aren't you going out then, Madge?"

Reg Pearce looked at his sister with distaste. What a drab piece she was, all pasty-faced and pimply.

"No."

Madge was slumped at one end of the small settee in the front room, watching a film on television and sucking a sweet. Her jaws moved rhythmically and her eyes followed James Mason. He was old now: even when that film was made he couldn't have been young, not really, but he was nice in a way. Watching him helped her not to think of her own miseries.

Maybe if he helped her a bit, Reg thought, she'd brace up. She didn't seem to have even any girl friends; if he took her out, someone might give her a few ideas about how to go on. He'd no definite plans for the evening — just the idea of going to the bowling alley or finding some of his mates around town. He'd decided to give Mick Green a wide berth; Mick wasn't serious about busting into Widnes' Stores, Reg was sure, but just in case he was, Reg didn't want to know. It was too close to his own doorstep.

"Like to come out with me?" he asked Madge now. "We could find a few of my mates, maybe."

Madge could only think that one of his mates was Mick Green.

"No, thanks, Reg," she said. "I don't go for your kind of crowd."

"Suit yourself." Reg felt snubbed but also relieved. "I certainly don't want to be lumbered with you, you ugly pudding," he said, and departed, whistling.

Their mother had heard this exchange.

"Oh Madge, why didn't you go with Reg?" she asked. "He'd look after you."

Madge had begun weeping at Reg's last remark.

"I don't like his mates — they're a rude lot," was all she could manage to say.

Norman left Felicity later than he intended. They had fallen asleep, and he had woken with a start and a rush of guilt. Gently he eased himself out of the bed, trying not to waken her, but she roused as he finished dressing and watched him with a soft tender expression on her face. He could do that to her — make her look like that, he thought with pride.

She reached out an arm to him and he kissed her.

"Till Thursday," he said.

Knowing nothing of the letter to Canada, which she finished after he left, Norman hurried along the road, crossed the railway and went up the path past Mrs Minter's house. It was almost eleven o'clock when he entered the square and walked over to the shop.

As soon as he opened the door into the lobby and felt the cold air whistling in through the broken glass in the back door, which had banged shut when Mick left, he knew that something had happened. Sick fear caught him in the stomach.

"Emma," he called, racing up the stairs. "Emma — I'm back, dear," and he entered her room.

As Mrs Costello still did not answer the telephone after the film ended, Mrs Minter crossed the square and rang the bell.

There was no answer at the door, either. Jane might be ill — she had been in a very low state earlier. On the other hand, she might merely be in bed, loaded with gin. There was nothing for it but to find out. She knew that the back door would have been left open for the wandering Pedro. Pausing only to go home and collect a torch, Mrs Minter was soon covering the same ground that Mick had gone over earlier. Like him, she saw Mrs Costello sleeping in her chair. She was snoring, and bending over her, Mrs Minter soon knew the cause of her slumber.

It was over an hour later when, having got her difficult, gin-sodden friend upstairs and into bed, Mrs Minter left by way of the front door, her mind full of the need to do something about the old woman. The squalor of Mrs Costello's bedroom had brought home to her the depths to which she had now sunk.

Across the square, outside Widnes' Stores, a police car was parked. Its blue light was turned off, and Mrs Minter paid little attention to it, supposing it to be a patrol keeping an eye on the local night life. Then a second police car, a dark saloon, drew up behind the first. As

Mrs Minter opened her own front door she saw two men in plain clothes get out and go over to the hardware shop.

Norman Widnes must have been burgled. How dreadful — just his luck; some people perpetually attracted misfortune.

She did not learn until the next morning the full horror of what had happened.

The scene in Emma's bedroom was grim enough to shock even the most hardened policeman. Detective Superintendent Beddoes and Detective Inspector Cudlipp from Muddington CID, summoned by the constable who had arrived after Norman's telephone call to the police, took in the details.

Emma's body lay sprawled, the face contused and battered, the skull crushed. A gash slit one cheek and her eyes stared glassily at them. There was blood on the bed-clothes and on the carpet, but there was no sign of the weapon that had done the damage. The wardrobe door hung open, but it was not until the police asked Norman where he kept his money that he realized the safe had gone.

He sat on an upright chair in the sitting-room telling the superintendent how he had found Emma, just as he had already told the uniformed constable who had arrived first. He had been to The Grapes and then for a walk, he said. He often went for walks. He had walked in the fields by the railway, and along the streets.

"In the dark?" asked the superintendent.

"Yes."

"Alone?"

"Yes."

"Till eleven o'clock?"

"Yes."

While he talked, Norman's heart pounded and there was a strange sort of humming in his ears. He had neither wept nor raged. He simply could not believe what had happened.

The police photographer arrived, and then the divisional surgeon. While they worked, Norman continued to sit in his chair, staring before him. He protested when he realized that they were going to take Emma away, wanting her to remain in her own bed at least for the night, as a mark of respect. It had to be like this, the superintendent said.

"There'll be no crowd to see her go now, Mr Widnes," said Detective Inspector Cudlipp. "It would be different by morning."

She was an awkward burden to get down the narrow staircase in death, as she had been in life two weeks before.

"What time did she die?" Norman asked at last, when it was done.

"We'll have to wait for the doctor to tell us that," said Detective Superintendent Beddoes.

But the body was cool already. The killer must have come and gone some time before Norman arrived home. Inquiries at the houses on each side of the shop had produced nothing. Detective Sergeant French said that two men in a flat over the greengrocer's shop were having their Ovaltine nightcap when he called; they had been listening to records most of the evening and had heard no unusual noise; there was always a fair amount of traffic along the road on a Saturday night. The single-storey newsagent's shop on Norman's other side was empty at night. The thief had chosen his target well, and since the safe had disappeared, he must have had some means of escape — a car parked in some side-street, for instance.

The full forensic investigation and detailed inquiries in the area were postponed until daylight, and Norman was told that he would have to leave the flat for what remained of the night.

"But why?" he asked. "I won't go into Emma's room — I understand that nothing must be touched."

He was desperate to be left alone: he needed solitude to absorb the frightful truth about what had happened; Norman had no instinct to turn outwards for comfort in disaster.

Cudlipp patiently explained that the thief might have left traces of his visit in other parts of the flat. The only obvious signs were in Emma's room and downstairs, where the break-in had occurred, but there might be fingerprints and other evidence elsewhere.

"Have you some friends where you could go?" he asked.

Norman had no time for friends and so had few of them. He thought of Mrs Bowling and her husband: he could not ask them in the middle of the night after such a terrible event; Mrs Bowling would be shocked enough when she heard the news as it was. Then he remembered kind Jack Phelps, who had taken Emma out for her last drive. Jack and his wife would take him in.

"We'll let you back as soon as we can, Mr Widnes," Cudlipp assured him when the horrified Phelps had instantly agreed.

Norman, alone at last in the Phelps' spare bedroom after they had spent more than an hour discussing the tragedy over cups of tea and brandy, did not even undress. He lay on the bed staring at the ceiling, thinking that Emma had been lying dead in the violated flat while he was with Felicity.

Meanwhile Mick Green had been drinking with Terry in The Rising Sun in New Bidbury and trying to look as if nothing unusual had happened. He knew, though, that he could never claim his bet.

But he'd got the loot, and what a lot; over five hundred pounds in cash. There'd been a wad of cheques too, which were a dead loss. But he'd never dreamed of finding such a sum of money. He could do plenty with that.

He felt no more regret for what he had done to Emma than for the death of the spaniel. Both were in the way and he had dealt with them.

CHAPTER
FIFTEEN

God did not listen to either Jamie or his father, and the sun shone brightly on Sunday morning. At breakfast Lydia chatted eagerly about their forthcoming outing, bobbing up and down from the table to attend to preparations for the picnic — boiling eggs, heating home-made soup, even finding time to bake fresh rolls.

Jamie grew quieter and quieter. He ate his *muesli* and apple, and obediently amused Claire while his father, who was firmly resigned now, went out to check the car. Leading Claire by the hand, Jamie, in desperation, pursued Geoffrey and suggested that his sister was getting a cold; perhaps they should put off their trip?

"Is she?" Geoffrey inspected his daughter, who teetered before him on stout limbs destined to develop as sturdily as her mother's. "Come on, Claire, let's look at you."

He held out his arms, and with a shriek of joy Claire cast herself adrift from Jamie and lurched over the space between them into his safe embrace. This was what life was all about, thought Geoffrey, his heart warmed by love for the plump child. He looked at Jamie, who was very pale and whose eyes behind his glasses were slightly pink. Weedy little boys could develop into stalwart men and it was his duty to support Lydia's plans for the children. She was a wonderful mother — sensible and never emotional; what was the use in being fey, like Sarah Armitage?

What on earth had made him think of Sarah like that? Geoffrey banished the image of her pale face and addressed his son.

"Claire's all right. She's teething," he said. If they put the trip off now, they would only have to do it another weekend instead. "It will do us all good to have a day out. Lend a hand there, will you, with the pump?"

He put Claire into the car where she would be safe and then, kind, affectionate father that he was, spent at least an extra ten minutes attending to the tyres so that Jamie might learn how to test pressures and work the footpump.

Lydia brought out rugs and the picnic basket. Then she took Claire away to get ready, telling Jamie to wash and put on his anorak.

Jamie followed her into the house. His father went into the cloakroom to wash the dirt and grease from his hands. Jamie took a deep breath. If his parents could just understand that he didn't like animals, surely they wouldn't waste their money giving him a dog? If he could explain it all to his grandmother, perhaps she would convince them. He went upstairs, collected his anorak but also emptied his piggy-bank of all his savings, seventy-five pence, then went into the kitchen where he found a carrier bag and piled into it apples, bananas and one of his mother's wholemeal loaves. There were no biscuits or sweets in this house. Then he was off, through the front door and running down the road as fast as he could.

Geoffrey, still in the cloakroom, never heard him go.

For Sunday breakfast Paula Curtis gave her daughter some milk and a slice of bread and dripping. Laura was hungry, so she ate it all up. Then, unaccustomed to such heavy food, her stomach revolted and she vomited.

Paula's instinct was to slap her and put her to bed. But it was a fine morning and she had arranged to take one of the bulldogs over to a breeder on the far side of the county with whose bitch he was to mate, so instead she followed the slap by wiping the vomit off the child with the dish-cloth, zipping her into her ski-suit and bundling her out to wait by the car, telling her to stay there while she shut the house and rounded up the dogs.

The telephone rang while she was locking the back door, and after a moment's hesitation she went in to answer it.

It was Guy. He wanted to see her to discuss the future and said he was coming over right away.

Paula was angry. He'd left it long enough if it was last weekend's episode that was on his mind. She didn't inquire about his activities and she expected the same treatment in return; besides, she did not want to change her arrangements for the day. He never considered her convenience, she told him, turning up without warning at any hour, so why should she now alter her plans because of a sudden whim of his? He must come another time.

She rang off, very annoyed. Things suited her this way, for Guy gave her enough money and seldom came

129

near her. Since his appearance last weekend Harry had not been back and that was another cause for resentment; Paula had not yet tired of Harry. She returned to the car with her mind distracted, and when Boris, the Labrador, did not answer her call she decided to go without him.

Her route did not go near the square, so she did not see the police, and had driven several miles before she realized that Laura, like the Labrador, had been left behind. Even then she did not immediately turn back for she was reluctant to abandon her plans. The child would be all right, damn her; she'd wander about the garden with Boris. They spent hours together every day and came to no harm.

In the end though, she did turn round, first stopping at a telephone box to let the owner of the bulldog bitch know she would be delayed.

At a quarter to nine Mrs Minter went across to see how Mrs Costello had survived the night and found part of the square cordoned off. Two police cars were parked outside the ironmonger's, and as she walked past she met Mrs Bowling, who was sobbing.

"Oh, isn't it dreadful, Mrs Minter?" she wept. "I can't hardly take it in. Poor, poor thing."

"Why? What's happened?" asked Mrs Minter. "I thought there must have been a burglary."

Mrs Bowling had heard the news from the paper-boy and had gone round to the shop at once. She had found Norman absent and the place full of police. A detective sergeant was about to call and question her, for Norman had told them that she worked there. Her fingerprints had to be eliminated from the various sets identified in the flat.

"Oh, how dreadful!" Mrs Minter exclaimed, when she had heard all this. "And Norman was out, was he?"

"Yes. He goes to The Grapes most Saturdays — never for long, mind you — devoted, he was — and then for a stroll. She was never left for long. I'd have gone in, if I'd been asked. Then she might still be alive," mourned Mrs Bowling. "I'll never forgive myself."

"It wasn't your fault," said Mrs Minter bluntly, "And if you had been there, you might have been attacked too."

This theory silenced Mrs Bowling, and Mrs Minter, trying to collect her own thoughts, went on to see Mrs Costello.

She found her friend up, dressed in a fawn woollen dressing-gown, bewilderedly watching the plainclothes policemen who were systematically inspecting what seemed to be every inch of her garden.

Heading for the bus stop, the first point on his journey to his grandmother, Jamie came into the square at a brisk trot. When he saw the police blocking the way he turned tail and fled back down Funnel Lane, heart pounding in fright. Like many a minor miscreant he was overcome by his own guilt at the sight of the law.

By instinct he padded blindly round the corner and into Foster Avenue; then he faltered, for the dog would be there.

But it wasn't. Miraculously the roads was clear. Jamie ran along it, but slowed when he reached the Alsatian's usual spot and looked up the drive. All was quiet.

The next house was empty. Blank windows stared out above the cupressus. Jamie was used to seeing the "For Sale" sign outside.

He had to hide somewhere. An empty house seemed a good place. When he found the conservatory door unlocked, as it had been left by a careless viewer the day before, he could not believe his luck.

The police soon found the safe in daylight. It lay in clump of rhubarb, where Mick had dropped it. Bloodstains, dry now, indicated the use to which it had been put, the lock had been broken with a large wrench taken from Norman's store-room. It too lay in the garden, and was taken away to be tested for fingerprints. The broken fencing and sets of footprints going in both directions showed the route of the intruder.

Mrs Costello, when she had drunk the strong coffee and eaten the toast insisted on by Mrs Minter, felt a little better. She stood in the garden and watched as the CID men patiently quartered the area. Mrs Minter had explained her own footprints leading from the gate. More, those of a man, were very distinct, and a detective was making a plaster cast of one of the sharpest. Fragments of clothing had been found on the fence between the greengrocer's garden and Norman's, and there was a strand of cotton thread on a bush near Mrs Costello's window.

"He stood here," said the policeman who had found it as he carefully sealed it in a polythene bag, and did not add, watching you, but Mrs Minter, looking at the scuffed ground nearby, understood.

"But killing Emma Widnes —" Mrs Costello kept repeating.

"Come along in, Jane, and have some more coffee," said Mrs Minter, unwilling to admit that she, too, felt so shocked that she needed some herself.

"Hooligans. Brutes. Beasts," said Mrs Costello, and then suddenly added. "I suppose it was the thief who killed her?"

"Of course it was," said Mrs Minter. "Who else could it have been?"

"Norman might have done it. I always thought he killed his mother," said Mrs Costello. "I told you so, too."

"Jane! For goodness' sake!" Mrs Minter, appalled, cast an anxious look at the young detective constable who was calmly continuing his search for clues among the shrubs. "That's nonsense. Come inside."

Mrs Costello allowed herself to be led indoors. Left alone, the policeman was thoughtful as he worked, and later he told Detective Sergeant French what the old woman had said.

As soon as Jamie was missed at home, Lydia went round to ask if either of the Armitages had seen him. Kenneth, who was just leaving for his bellringing stint before morning service, said he would look out for Jamie and departed, astonished that a woman as well organized as Lydia should have mislaid a child.

"It's extraordinary," Lydia said. "I can't understand where he's got to — we'd planned this lovely trip to the safari park and he was longing to go."

"Was he?" Sarah asked.

"Of course."

Lydia was not yet worried, just cross and puzzled.

They searched the Armitages' garage and garden shed, and stood on the tiny lawn calling him by name, but in vain. Geoffrey, meanwhile had inquired at the other houses in the close and then taken the car to search the neighbouring roads. After Lydia had gone home, Sarah saw him return alone; she picked up Simon and went round to see what they planned to do next.

"There's been some trouble in the square," Geoffrey said. "There are several police cars up there. I think someone has broken into Widnes' Stores."

"Did you ask the police if they'd seen Jamie?" Sarah asked.

Geoffrey hadn't. It seemed too soon to take what was just a naughty prank so seriously.

"We'll give him half an hour," he said "Then, if he's not back, we must do that. I'll go round the roads again."

Sarah did not see that there was anything to be gained by delay; as he left in the car she knew that in their place she would have been frantic.

"Well, at least there's no rubbish tip nearby where he might have got into an old refrigerator," she said, and at this Lydia did show some anxiety.

"You don't really think anything can have happened to him, do you, Sarah?" she asked.

"No, of course not," said Sarah. "He's just hiding somewhere. He'll turn up when he's hungry."

But she did not altogether believe it.

By this time the church bells were adding their clangour to the growing tension.

"Damn that bloody noise," said Geoffrey, returning. He now looked very worried. "You'll have to know what's happened," he added. "Mrs Widnes is dead. There was a robbery at the shop last night and whoever did it killed her. I've told the police about Jamie and they're sending someone round."

The police constable to whom Geoffrey had somewhat sheepishly told his story had taken it very seriously. He had gone into the shop and emerged with an older man in plain clothes who, after hearing what Geoffrey had to say, sent him home to find a photograph of the boy and be ready to make a formal statement. As Geoffrey left, a message was already being relayed to police headquarters.

"They'll soon find him," Sarah said. "He can't be far away."

Lydia had been to Jamie's room making sure his anorak had gone. "He took his piggy-bank money," she said. "He might have caught a bus."

Or hitched a lift.

Soon after nine that morning, Detective Inspector Cudlipp and Detective Sergeant French called to question Madge. Though they were in plain clothes, Mrs Pearce knew at once that they were policemen and her first thought was that Reg had had an accident with the motor-bike. He was still asleep upstairs, it was true, but he might have hit something on his way home last night. It couldn't be anything to do with Harry; for once, she had known all his movements for the past twenty-four hours, and he had even taken her out for a drink the evening before. He was already in the garden raking over the seed-bed, the model of domestic rectitude. It wouldn't last, but while it did she meant to make the most of it.

So when the police asked for Madge, she was astonished.

"We'd better come in, if you don't mind, Mrs Pearce," said the inspector, who was a thickset man of about her own age, with a craggy face and prominent pale blue eyes.

"Well, of course."

Madge had been finishing her breakfast in the kitchen. She had not eaten much, just a few cornflakes, and she came into the living-room yawning, hiding her mouth with her hand.

"Well now, Madge," said the inspector. "You work at Widnes' Stores, don't you?"

Madge nodded. The world began to spin. Here it came.

"Would you mind telling me where you were last night? Between nine and ten o'clock?"

Madge managed to answer.

"Here. Watching telly," she uttered.

"That's right — she was here all evening," said Mrs Pearce, edging protectively forward. What a question to ask. What could be behind it? "There was that James Mason film. Why do you want to know?"

"I'm afraid I've got some bad news for you," Cudlipp said.

Mick had done it: he had busted into the shop; the waiting was over.

"The premises were raided last night. Money was stolen and Mrs Widnes is dead."

Madge heard the first words. As she fainted, she thought she imagined the rest.

Her mother, bending to tend the lumpy body of her fallen daughter, was thinking that in fact Madge had been alone in the house during the film, for she and Harry had been at the pub. The girl wasn't involved, of course, and no one would suspect for a moment that she was; but on the other hand her presence at home couldn't be proved.

When Kenneth had finished his bellringing and the worshippers were safely inside the church, he stopped in the square on the way home to find out what was going on.

His face, when he returned, was grave, but there was no one there to witness his solemn entrance. Nor was there any smell of roasting meat.

Impatiently, he went round next door, where he found his wife with Lydia and Geoffrey in the kitchen, untouched cups of coffee before them, and the two small children crawling round their feet. His role of informant was rudely snatched from him as he was told all that was known, and of the visit of a woman police constable to take particulars of Jamie's disappearance. She had only just gone. Barely waiting for the tale to be done, Kenneth seized his chance to be alarmist.

"I don't want to upset you," he said, desiring to do just that. "But you must be ready to face a most serious situation. A murderer may be at large in the district.

Whoever killed Mrs Widnes must be insane. If he met Jamie wandering about he may have abducted him to use as a hostage."

"Oh no," said Geoffrey at once. "He'd be miles away by now. People who assault helpless women don't — don't kidnap little boys."

"There was no need to attack Mrs Widnes," Kenneth pointed out. "She couldn't have prevented the robbery. There's a maniac at large, but you must do your best to keep calm."

The house smelled funny: damp and musty. Jamie wrinkled his nose and shivered. He would have to wait for a bit — till it was dark — before he could set out for his grandmother's. He was sure he had enough money for the bus, though it was quite a long way; it took nearly three hours by car. You went to Muddington to start with, and then to Gloucester. He recited her address to himself. It was lucky he'd thought of the food; he needn't be hungry while he waited. Jamie was very conscious of the need for regular nourishment since the preparation of wholesome meals took up so much of his mother's attention.

The conservatory was not a very interesting place. He opened the door that led into the house beyond, and went in somewhat timidly, but there was nothing to be seen except empty rooms. His confidence grew as he investigated; most of the doors were open and he had no fear of something nasty lurking to pounce. The floor, dusty boards, creaked here and there as Jamie walked along. The stairs had dark edges and pale centres, where the treads had been stained on either side of a carpet strip. The bath was funny, on feet, and with an orange mark under the taps. He tried the water, but only a few brownish drops emerged.

From one of the bedrooms he looked out over the garden. It was wild, like a forest, full of trees and bushes. He'd go and explore. There might be food — nuts or fruit. He decided to make his headquarters in the biggest bedroom where there was a fireplace and a window seat, and he dumped his plastic carrier of provisions there. It was at the back, away from the road, although that was not something he took into account. Then he went out into the garden.

There was a lot of long grass, still dew-laden, and his shoes and socks soon got wet. There were fruit bushes, but no fruit at this time of year. There were old windfall apples on the ground, however; most were eaten away or rotten, but some were still sound. He ate one to be going on with, luckily chancing to choose a sweet one.

Then he beheld a terrible sight.

He had come through the trees into a clearing, and before him was a pond. A little child, much the size of his own sister, was standing in the water and a big black dog seemed to be trying to eat her.

Jamie then acted, within his own terms of reference, with courage equal to that of any holder of the Victoria Cross. He sped over the grass, small face set, eyes blazing behind his spectacles, and with one hand pushed at the dog in an effort to get him away from the child, while at the same time hauling her out of the shallow water with the other.

"Go away, go away," he hissed at Boris.

Boris, thankful for help in his attempt to save Laura from her own recklessness, relinquished his grip on her clothing and turned to Jamie with a delighted grin on his whiskered face. His tail wagged to and fro and he snuffled with pleasure.

Jamie's heart was beating so hard that he felt it would thump its way right out of his chest. The dog did not seem to be attacking him, but nevertheless he still tried to shoo Boris off. Laura had begun to cry; she was accustomed to Boris's methods, and now looked from him to Jamie in perplexity, not used to comfort from a human.

"There, there, little girl." Jamie had no doubt that the bedraggled creature was female. "Don't cry. We'll go into the house, you'll be safe there, and then you can tell me where you live." For this empty house could not be her home. "What's your name?"

But Laura was unable to say. She allowed him to take her hand, though, and they trotted off together up the garden, Boris following behind. Jamie cast anxious glances over his shoulder at the black dog, but he certainly did not seem savage. He had heard of dogs rescuing humans; Saint Bernards, for instance. It dawned on him that the dog could have been trying to pull Laura out of the water.

By the time they reached the house he was scarcely afraid of Boris at all; he was nicer to look at than Gyp,

140

not so tall, though fatter, and his coat was smooth. He had a kind face, too, while Gyp's was a curious box-shaped one with a squared-off jaw.

Boris followed the children into the house and up the stairs, which Laura took ages to climb, step by step, hanging on to Jamie. He realized that she must be older than Claire, who could not stand for long alone; this little girl could walk properly and was taller, though she was skinny-looking. She had stopped crying.

"Lie down, boy," instructed Jamie when they reached his headquarters, and Boris obeyed.

Jamie felt a surge of power. He was a king, with a kingdom and two subjects. He pulled off Laura's wet boots; her socks and trouser ends were very wet, and so was her bottom. He sighed; Claire was like that too. Solemnly he undressed her down to her vest and sweater and spread her wet garments out to dry, then put her back into her ski-suit minus her damp, grey pants.

She rubbed her eyes and said, "Boy."

Jamie was delighted.

"I'm Jamie," he said. "What's your name?" She might answer now.

But Laura had exhausted her vocabulary.

She could be hungry. He gave her a banana, peeling it for her and breaking it into pieces which he fed her one by one, as his mother did with Claire. Laura wolfed it down. Perhaps she would go to sleep, he thought; Claire slept a good deal. He cast about for a bed. There was nothing in the room so he took off his own anorak, coaxed her to sit on it and wrapped it round her. Boris, who had been lying perfectly still while all this went on, now got up and sidled over to the children.

Jamie panicked for a moment but did not show it beyond a tremble in his voice as he stoutly said, "Good boy," and waited to see what would happen.

Laura put her hand on the dog's neck and he settled down beside her. She leant against him, grubby cheek on his coat, and began to suck a grimy finger. Both lay still.

She seemed all right. Jamie decided to have a look round the house for anything to add to their comfort. There might be a rug somewhere, or at least a sack. He walked all over the house once more this time looking in cupboards. He found a pile of old newspapers and thought that if only he had a match he could light a fire; there was plenty of wood in the garden. There were some old curtains bundled in a cupboard in the scullery; they smelled rather nasty, but they were better than nothing, so he carted them upstairs. They'd do as coverings or to lie on. Then, just to be on the safe side, he went down and bolted the doors through which they had entered the house.

A police constable, coming along the drive a little later looking for the missing boy, tried the doors and found them bolted. He checked the ground-floor windows and looked in the outhouses and garage, but saw no trace of occupancy nor any sort of disturbance.

Jamie, upstairs, saw him and crouched down out of sight, an anxious eye on Laura and Boris in case they made a noise, but they were silent. Soon the policeman went away.

CHAPTER
SIXTEEN

Madge's faint lasted for only seconds. Before long she was sitting on the settee allowing her fingerprints to be taken, while her mother made some fresh tea.

She answered Detective Inspector Cudlipp's questions in a flat voice.

Yes, she did know where the money was kept.

She knew who had taken it, too, and who had killed Mrs Widnes, and she wanted to tell the policeman, but her throat closed and she could not do it. And perhaps it wasn't Mick after all; perhaps he'd told someone else about the safe and they'd done the job. For would even Mick have done such a dreadful thing as a murder?

She remembered his hands, and his hard, cruel words, and she knew that he would.

Although she could not follow a religion in whose name fearful inquisitions had been held and bloody wars raged, and which was still an excuse for bigotry and violence, Mrs Minter admired the architecture and the music it had inspired and would never question the faith of others. Accordingly she encouraged Mrs Costello to stick to her routine and go to church that morning. It would keep her occupied for an hour, and out of the way of the police.

Muttering that this murder business would interfere with the search for Pedro, Mrs Costello departed, wearing the wreck of a persian lamb coat and with her wild hair tethered under a scarf.

Mrs Minter went home to prepare lunch for her guests; despite what had happened, one had to eat, but she expected her party to be somewhat glum. She was laying the table when the doorbell rang.

One of the policemen she had seen earlier stood on the step: a balding man with sandy hair, in plain clothes.

"Detective Sergeant French, madam. Could I have a word?" he asked.

She let him in, and saw him cast a swift glance round; his expression, however, remained impassive.

"About Mrs Costello," he began. "Rather an — er — excitable lady, would you say?"

"She's upset at present, sergeant. Her dog disappeared yesterday."

"Ah — I heard about that. Unfortunate. Ladies get attached to their pets."

He looked about, expecting there to be one here too.

"I haven't got a dog, sergeant," said Mrs Minter. "There are far too many of them about as it is."

"Quite. Well — Detective Constable Adams heard Mrs Costello refer to the death of Mrs Widnes senior — the mother of Mr Norman Widnes, that is. Before I ask Mrs Costello just what she meant, I thought I would see if you could explain."

"It was a thoughtless remark and best forgotten," said Mrs Minter promptly. Now what had Jane started?

"I can easily check up on when Mrs Widnes senior died, Mrs Minter, and in what circumstances, but it would save time if you would tell me what you know. You've lived in Old Bidbury some time, I believe."

"Twelve years. Well — anyone will tell you — Mrs Widnes was ill for a long time and suffered a great deal." Mrs Minter paused.

"Yes — well, she was ill?" French prompted.

"In the end she died suddenly. Mrs Costello very foolishly said that her son might have given her some sort of overdose."

"Had she grounds for such an allegation ?"

"None at all. Mr Widnes was devoted to his mother and he was just as devoted to his wife," said Mrs Minter firmly. "I'm very sorry for him, poor man."

"His wife was a helpless invalid?"

"Almost helpless. She could move about a little. She was in no pain. She read, and played cards, and watched what went on in the square from her window." Mrs Minter looked sharply at the sergeant. "I don't know what's in your mind, but I've heard that Emma Widnes was hit over the head. Norman would never do anything so cruel. If you think there's something in Mrs Costello's silly remark about his mother's death, and that having done it once he then helped Emma along too, you're quite wrong. Her killing must have been a brutal business. You're looking for a thief, aren't you? Someone who has committed robbery with violence — violence ending in murder."

"We're looking for a thief, yes," said French.

But what if Norman had come in, found the place ransacked, and seized the chance to get rid of his fat, ugly wife, throwing the blame on the burglar? If such an outrageous thought could enter her own mind, Mrs Minter realized, the sergeant was capable of having it too. But perhaps he did not know about Felicity.

In fact French thought that the flaw in this theory was Norman's affection for his wife, which was emphasized by everyone; he appeared to have no motive at all for wanting to be rid of her, and it was certainly no mercy killing.

Police inquiries in the neighbourhood went on methodically throughout the morning. No one seemed to have heard or seen anything unusual.

The landlord at The Grapes confirmed that Norman had been in the night before. He stayed not much above five minutes, had a beer, bought a bottle of wine and left: his normal Saturday pattern.

"Was he going straight home?" enquired Detective Sergeant French.

"Why not ask him?" parried the landlord.

French was thinking that if he, himself, went out walking for a couple of hours he would prefer not to carry a bottle of wine around with him.

"Thought he might have mentioned it. Took a bottle back to the wife every weekend, did he? *After* the evening meal?"

"Perhaps it was for Sunday?" suggested the landlord.

He knew Norman didn't go straight home, and hoped his guess about what he was up to was right; he didn't know who the woman was, and he wasn't going to put the idea into the heads of the police — or of anyone else, come to that. The poor bastard had had a raw deal all round and didn't need his troubles adding to. It wasn't as if he could have had anything whatever to do with last night's dreadful business.

Emma's death was reported on the radio at one o'clock. Felicity began to pay attention only when she heard the words "Old Bidbury".

". . . robbery, near Muddington," said the announcer. "A hardware shop in the town was robbed, and the owner's wife was attacked. Mrs Widnes an invalid who was aged forty-nine, is dead . . ." The BBC did not yet know that further drama had struck Old Bidbury and two children were missing.

Felicity sat down, feeling suddenly giddy.

"Felicity! What's wrong? You look as if you'd seen a ghost!" exclaimed Elsie Dawes, who had invited herself to lunch, a thing she often did on Sundays, and then, "Oh — the news — didn't you know? The square is swarming with police. I thought you'd have heard."

"I hadn't," said Felicity faintly.

"Well, it's ghastly, of course. Poor old bag — she was bashed on the head, I believe," said Elsie. "Not a friend of yours, was she?"

"I had met her," said Felicity. God, how awful!

"Rather a bloody business," said Elsie.

Felicity could eat no lunch. Afterwards, at Elsie's suggestion, they went out in the car to visit a stately home. On the way, Felicity posted her letter to the Canadian school.

"And so your opinion is?" inquired Detective Superintendent Beddoes.

He and Detective Inspector Cudlipp had been going through the statements about last night's crime. Cudlipp had passed on the hearsay from Mrs Costello about Norman's mother.

"I think, like Mrs Minter — a reliable sort of woman, French says — that it's wild gossip on the part of an eccentric old soul who's upset at the loss of her dog," said Cudlipp. "But I'll have a word with the doctor. It's the same one — Dr Barrett — who'd been looking after the second Mrs Widnes."

"Do that," agreed Beddoes. "Everyone seems of the opinion that Widnes was a devoted husband," he added.

"Yes, sir."

"What do you think?"

"There's been no suggestion at all otherwise," said Cudlipp. "But what a strange pair."

"She didn't always look like that, Fred, and for better or worse, you know. I've seen stranger attachments. He may have still pictured her in his mind as she was once — handsome, according to the photographs we saw. And he was certainly shocked when we got there."

"True enough." Cudlipp began gathering the papers together. "Well, if we can get any sort of lead to the villain, we should get something on him from forensic. There were the footprints and the bits of his clothing. And he might have picked up some wisps of blanket, not to mention blood."

"Widnes could have faked the whole thing," said the superintendent slowly.

"Oh no, sir. His footprints don't match up. Though he'd time. No alibi since he left the pub. Walking around with a bottle of wine for over three hours — a likely tale."

"Of course he wasn't walking around all that time," said Beddoes. "He's got a woman. That was probably how he managed to stay devoted to his wife."

Cudlipp reflected, as often before, that his own cynicism was only exceeded by that of his superior. Both had seen too much of the misery that could fester under an apparently untroubled surface.

"There's Madge Pearce," Cudlipp said. "The girl who works in the shop. Her prints were on the safe."

"But Widnes didn't think she knew about it, did he?" Beddoes said.

"That's right, sir. It seems she did errands for Mrs Widnes, though — fetched things for her, like shoes from the wardrobe. That was how she saw it."

"What sort of girl is she?"

"Very plain, sir, and spotty. She passed out when she heard what had happened. Only sixteen," said Cudlipp.

"She's not the lady in the case, then."

Cudlipp's face showed what he thought of this flight of fancy.

"Could she have been an accomplice of the villain?"

"I doubt it," said Cudlipp. "No boy friends, her mother said — not that sort of girl at all."

Surely most girls were that sort, thought Beddoes.

"Well, bear it in mind," he said mildly. "And see what you can find out about Widnes's side activities."

The Widnes tragedy dominated Mrs Minter's lunch-party conversation.

"But did you know that Jamie Renshaw has disappeared?" said Rose Hallam, when the first flurry of talk about the killing had died down. The Hallams were among those Geoffrey had called on to ask if they had seen him.

"Derek disappeared once," said Mrs Minter. "When we were going to do something he didn't want to do — he hid until it was too late to go. It was very frightening. I was furious."

"Jamie's a funny little boy," said Rose. "Geoffrey said he's scared of dogs — Norman Widnes had been taking him to school for over a week, it seems, to avoid some Alsatian he meets on the way."

This talk of dogs upset Mrs Costello again, and she went into a new lament about Pedro.

"What's happening to Bidbury?" she cried. "First Pedro — then Emma Widnes — now Jamie Renshaw. Who'll be next?"

Mrs Minter thought these disasters varied in degree. She said so, and added that Pedro might reappear, and Jamie certainly would.

"Things do go in threes, don't they, though?" said Rose.

"Let's hope not, or not to a pattern," said Bob. "I hope you're right about Jamie, Kitty. But suppose he hitched a lift with someone — he could be miles away by now."

150

All through the roast pork they speculated about where Jamie might be.

"At least he didn't disappear from outside school, enticed away by a stranger with sweets," said Rose.

She was clearly very upset by Jamie's disappearance, and as she helped Mrs Minter to clear away the dishes, told her in the kitchen about the dinner party at the Armitages.

"I had to tell them about Norman. Just in case," she said, wanting Kitty Minter's assurance that she could not have been in any way to blame for what had happened.

Norman sat with his head in his hands staring at the carpet. Brown and orange swirls meandered over a darker brown background. He had never liked it.

What now? The police were still busy down in the shop and storeroom, though they had finished upstairs. He supposed they would find the killer in the end. It was strange that none of Emma's jewellery had gone; she had several quite valuable rings, but her dressing-table drawer hadn't been touched. Norman thought thieves always looked there first. What had made this one go to the wardrobe? It was almost as though he knew where to find the money. Perhaps he had forced Emma to tell him where it was, before he killed her.

As he sat there, Mrs Bowling came in, having heard that he was back. Because she did not know what to say to him, she put the kettle on to make some tea, plugging it in just as Emma had always done, near the sofa, then clucking to herself and bearing it off to the kitchen, the proper place for boiling kettles. There was no longer any point in hiding Emma's food supplies, and she put some cake and four custard cream biscuits on the tray when she took the tea to him.

"You must keep up your strength," she said, pouring them each a cup.

She'd been crying, Norman saw. She'd been very fond of Emma. Everyone who knew her had been fond of her.

One spouse may not give evidence against another. Well, that was over now. The secret, guarded in silence for so long, was safe for ever.

"You're not the only one in trouble," Mrs Bowling said, as they sipped their tea. "Though I expect he'll soon turn up."

"Who will?"

"Young Jamie Renshaw. He's gone missing."

CHAPTER
SEVENTEEN

"Laura — where are you?" called Paula, and added, "Damn the child," when there was no answer. She had expected to find Laura and Boris in some corner of the garden but there was no sign of either of them.

The gate had been left open; they could have wandered into the road.

Paula was cross. The thought that Laura might have had an accident did not enter her mind. She regarded the child as an ill-behaved puppy which still urinated where it shouldn't and had not yet learned to come to heel. For a few weeks after her birth Paula had felt a primitive affection for her, but when she cried or needed tending this soon wore off; now she was just another animal to be looked after, and one that gave Paula more trouble than any of the dogs.

Boris was Guy's dog, not hers.

Guy had been annoyed when, on the telephone, she had refused to see him. She didn't know where he was speaking from. He could have come over, found the dog and the child on their own and taken them both off, just to spite her. Well, she'd give him no satisfaction. He could get on with it. When Laura had whined and wet herself a few times, he'd bring her back; in fact, she didn't really mind if he kept her, but he wouldn't — she'd be too much trouble.

She telephoned the bulldog bitch's owner again and announced that she could bring her own dog over, after all.

When their mother was out of earshot, Madge, who had been very quiet ever since the detectives' visit, asked her brother where Mick Green lived.

Reg immediately made some snide comments and she had to endure baiting as to why she wanted to know before he would tell her.

"He's not your style, Madge," he said. This was what came of Mick taking the trouble to bring her home the other night; now she was stuck on him. Well, if she went to see him she'd soon get snubbed for her pains.

"I've got a message for him from a friend of mine," Madge said, her pallid face filling with colour as she told the lie.

All morning she'd been determining her action. If she saw him, she might know whether he looked guilty or not. Better still, she might discover that he was in bed with flu, or something, so that he couldn't possibly have done it. She thought she would be safe from him herself, in daylight. Besides, his mum and dad would be at his place. She imagined them as solid citizens, like her own parents, who had their preferences but presented a united, authoritative front to their children.

She didn't know what she would say to him if he was there.

154

But he wasn't, when she called that afternoon.

The door was opened by a thin little woman with wispy greying hair who looked very frail. She also looked very surprised at seeing Madge. Other girls had been round asking for Mick in the past, but none were like this one.

She told Madge that he'd gone out on the bike. She didn't know where, nor when he'd be back.

Madge walked away towards the park in the centre of New Bidbury. Daffodils were in bud, and the trees were pale with opening blossom; children ran about and pregnant mothers let their coats fly open, away from their distended stomachs. Madge sat on a bench feeling sour and wretched: everything was terrible and she was sick at heart thinking of the tragedy for which she was, in her own mind, responsible.

She went home at last, to be greeted by a hug from her mother and a slice of freshly baked sponge cake.

"That'll make you feel better, dear," said Edna, all concern, for Madge did look ill. "Maybe you'd better not go to the shop tomorrow. It'll hardly open, as it is."

"I'll have to," said Madge. "Mr Widnes may need help."

She couldn't just stay away, without a word; he might be counting on her.

After tea, seizing a moment when she was alone in the living-room, she took a sheet of notepaper and an envelope from the drawer where her mother kept them and went up to her room, where she wrote a short letter in large, uneven capitals. Then she went along to the post office, bought some stamps from the machine and

155

posted it. She did not realize that there would be no collection from the box till the next morning.

On Saturday night, after finding his friends, Mick had spent a lively time. They'd gone to Muddington with some girls. He'd flashed some of the money he'd stolen around a bit and that had won him the best bird; they'd ended up in a field on the way home — the very spot where he'd stopped with Madge. It made him laugh to think of that. This one was a bit different; though the field was chilly it had been very satisfactory. It was well into the early hours of Sunday morning before he got home; he felt no sense of guilt, and slept soundly.

Mick had grown up in the council flat in New Bidbury where he still lived. As a small boy he'd played on the scuffed grass in front of the block; later he'd haunted the streets and alleys around, with never enough to do in his spare time. His mother worked in a supermarket and his father in a factory, where at present he was on night shift.

On Sunday morning his mother brought him a cup of tea in bed, as she always did at weekends, because it helped to put him in a good mood and she was afraid of him. As he drank it, Mick remembered that he had killed a woman. She must be dead. No one could survive such an injury.

At the time he'd panicked for an instant; then, calm had returned. He had picked up the safe in his gloved hands, taken it downstairs, found a wrench in the store and broken it open out in the garden, by the light of his torch which he'd propped on a stone. He'd hurled the safe away from him into the darkness. At no time could anything have been seen from the road in front of the shop.

His friends, and particularly the girl he'd got hold of, wouldn't remember what time he'd joined them even if the fuzz did get around to asking. They'd say he'd been with them all night. There was nothing to link him with the crime at all: except Madge.

He finished his tea and got up. The radio was on but the news was long since over. He couldn't ask his mother if the killing had been reported.

"Well, Mick, going out today, are you?" his mother asked. When she looked at Mick she felt amazement that something so large and full of vitality could have had its beginnings within her own frail body.

"I'll please myself," said Mick. "And I'll have some more tea. Are my eggs ready?"

As the major contributor to the household budget he expected, and got, servility from her.

"Just coming," said his mother, flustered. Sundays were the worst problem in her difficult week, for if Mick were at home he played records loudly or watched telly, disturbing his father, and the two would often have a row. Several times they'd nearly had punch-ups; but Mick was bigger than his father, who had an ulcer and was a whiner, and got the best of things without using blows. Mick's sister had married and left the district at the first opportunity, so that Mrs Green was left fighting a lonely battle between the two men. "Had a nice evening, then, did you?" she asked Mick, sliding rashers, eggs and sausages on to a plate.

"What's it to you?" growled Mick, taking the plate without any thanks.

"I only asked," said Mrs Green.

"Keep your nose out of my affairs," said Mick.

His mother did not answer. She took the pan to the sink and made a great business of washing up. Silly cow, thought Mick, hearing the clatter. He'd only to open his mouth and she squirmed.

He spent the morning tinkering with his motor-bike and came back into the flat just in time to hear the one .o'clock news on the radio. When he heard the announcer's grave voice telling the world about the death of Emma Widnes, Mick felt amazement that he should have provoked so important an item.

He left the flat the moment the meal was over and went off on the bike. He must see Madge — he'd tell her the crime had nothing to do with him and she must forget about their conversation — it had all been a lark. However, if she did try to shop him no one would believe the silly bint — there was no evidence — it would be her word against his. There was nothing to worry about; he'd just chat her up a bit — she might be upset still, or else she might be beginning to hanker for a bit more of the same, in which case he'd give it her.

When he reached Madge's house she was out. Reg was there, though, and he told Mick that she'd asked for his address. They joked about it. Then Reg told him that Madge was pretty cut up about what had happened at the shop.

"Lucky it was just a joke about you giving it a going over, Mick," said Reg, relieved to find that Mick was quite his normal self, which he wouldn't have been if he'd been mixed up in something like that.

"Cor — yes," agreed Mick. "Good thing I didn't try it at the same time as that other fellow."

They left together, Reg roaring up the road behind Mick, who was wondering exactly why Madge should have wanted to know where he lived.

He'd have to fix her, that was for sure.

Detective Inspector Cudlipp found Dr Barrett in his garden, working a hoe through the ground where he planned to sow early peas. Though he had not been called to Emma in the night, the doctor knew what had happened to his patient.

Cudlipp asked about her general condition and Dr Barrett confirmed what the inspector already guessed: that her heart might have failed at any time; that she could have had another stroke; or that she might have lived for years, though her ever-increasing bulk was against her.

"She'd come to terms with her condition. She was content, in a limited way," said the doctor. "Lucky to have such a good husband. What a terrible way to die."

"What about Mr Widnes' mother? You looked after her too, didn't you?" asked Cudlipp.

"Yes, I did."

Dr Barrett told Cudlipp that the arrival of Emma had transformed Mrs Widnes' last months. Norman had done all that a man could to make his mother comfortable, but Emma had proved an excellent nurse.

"You expected her death?"

"It was inevitable but one never knows quite what to expect in these cases," said Dr Barrett.

"She did die naturally?" Cudlipp asked.

Dr Barrett looked at him over the top of his half-spectacles.

"What are you suggesting, Inspector? That I helped her?"

"Not you, no," said Cudlipp.

"Who, then? Not Norman?"

"Why not? Out of pity, you understand, though it's still a crime."

The doctor leaned on his hoe and surveyed the inspector thoughtfully.

"I don't think so," he said. "If he did, it was a merciful act, but no, I think not. I signed the death certificate."

"It's not impossible."

"No. But very unlikely."

"Why do you say that?"

Dr Barrett answered at once.

"It would be too positive an action for Norman Widnes. He's kind, but he lacks drive, dynamism, what you will. He's not one to strike out for himself."

"I'm not suggesting that this was for himself — it was for his mother," said Cudlipp.

"For himself too. He was tied."

"Well, he's free now," said Cudlipp. "I wonder what he'll do with his liberty."

"Find himself another cage, I imagine," said Dr Barrett. "People's natures don't change, you know."

After their belated lunch on Sunday, Kenneth took Gyp for a walk. He had not been gone long before Geoffrey came round, and Sarah, who had stayed at home in case the Renshaws needed help, saw at once that there was still no news of Jamie.

"The police ought to be hunting for him, not the murderer," she said. "He's alive, after all. It's too late to help poor Emma Widnes."

"I expect they can handle more than one case at a time," said Geoffrey mildly. Then he added, in a voice that Sarah could hardly bear, "We *believe* he's alive."

"Oh Geoff, of course he is! You mustn't even think of anything else," said Sarah.

"Well — suppose that freaky theory of Kenneth's about holing up isn't so freaky after all. Suppose by some odd chance Jamie had found the murderer hiding out somewhere."

"The timing's all wrong for anything like that," said Sarah. "The murder was last night. Whoever did it will be miles away from here by now. Jamie's only been missing a few hours. He'll soon be found, you'll see."

"It's awful to be so helpless," said Geoffrey. "Lydia's sitting right by the phone. I had to get out for a few minutes."

He supposed that Lydia's constant criticism of Sarah as disorganized was just, but he liked a bit of disorder himself. Now that Kenneth was out — Geoffrey had seen him go — Sarah had somehow rendered the usually rather antiseptic-seeming sitting-room into a homlier place merely by having some knitting lying on a chair and a crumpled *Observer* on the floor. Kenneth would never leave a newspaper in any other condition than pristine. Despite his anxiety, Geoffrey smiled at Sarah, sank down in the chair facing her, stretched out his legs, and sighed, "God, that's better."

Sarah could not think what he meant.

"Would you like some coffee?" she asked.

"Yes, please," said Geoffrey. "I couldn't eat any lunch. We nibbled at our picnic — wholemeal bread and cottage cheese."

"Our roast lamb wasn't ready on time," said Sarah. "And the potatoes were hard."

"Why worry?" said Geoffrey.

You try saying that to Kenneth, thought Sarah. She went through to the kitchen and rattled about. Geoffrey heard her drop a cup and swear, and he went out to see what had happened.

"Broken?" he asked.

"Yes, damn it."

"Best Rockingham?"

"No. Cornish ware from Widnes' Stores," said Sarah.

"Get another. No need to confess," said Geoffrey.

"I'm terribly clumsy," said Sarah.

"I think you're terribly sweet," said Geoffrey.

He put his arms round her and gently kissed her mouth. Sarah leaned against him, aware of Arran jersey and a comforting solidity. Then he let her go, and she spooned out their instant coffee.

"What about Jamie?" she asked in a practical voice when they were sitting down again. She would have liked to sit next to him on the sofa, and she would

162

have liked him to kiss her again. Being enfolded in Geoffrey's arms was not in the least like submitting to Kenneth's passionate onslaughts. "Is there really nothing we can do?"

"Nothing. We must leave it to the police," said Geoffrey. "I've got a feeling this dog business is at the bottom of it all — or the animal thing, I should say. You realized that he doesn't like dogs. The way to cure him isn't to thrust them at him. He needs gentle treatment." He thought for a minute and then added, "Like you."

Sarah kept calm. The wisest course was to ignore that last remark.

"Need he get to like dogs at all?" she asked. "After all, people don't get over disliking tapioca pudding."

"Fears should be overcome," said Geoffrey firmly. "Especially needless ones."

"Dogs don't hurt. They can bite," said Sarah, but she had a sudden feeling that they weren't really talking about dogs and Jamie any longer.

After their lunch with Mrs Minter, Rose and Bob Hallam decided against calling on the Renshaws with offers of help for fear of being intrusive; telephone inquiries, too, would merely block the lines. They went straight back to their house and were greeted rapturously by the dachshunds.

Bob watched Rose as she caressed them. She wore a smart bottle green outfit she'd been able to buy at a considerable discount as a staff perk from Marguerite's; her hair was slightly dishevelled and her usually pale face faintly flushed from the good meal and the wine.

What if they'd had a child who went missing? He knew that Rose would be frantic if one of the dachshunds disappeared; she seemed almost as sorry for Mrs Costello over the loss of her spaniel as she was for the Renshaws. But a dog could soon be replaced with another which at least would look the same. You couldn't replace a lost child.

The revulsion about the way she cuddled her dogs, which he had suppressed for years, suddenly overcame his tolerance. He'd had enough of them; her obsession with them wasn't healthy.

"Come to bed, Rose," he said abruptly.

She gaped at him.

"What — now? But it's half past three —"

It was years since they'd made love at such an hour.

"What's wrong with that? Gives us plenty of time," said Bob robustly.

Whatever would people think if they noticed drawn bedroom curtains in the middle of Sunday afternoon, at their age, Rose wondered.

"Well," she said, and giggled.

She put the dogs out first for a run in the garden.

While he went prospecting, Jamie shut Laura and Boris into the big bedroom together; they could not escape for Laura was too small to open the door. Jamie knew all about the dangers of stairs to small children.

He found a tea chest in the garage and carried it upstairs; though it wasn't very heavy, it was big and awkward for him to handle; it would be useful as a table. Then he brought in a supply of apples from the orchard;

164

with his other storage, they would feed him and the little girl until they could get to his grandmother's. This had now become his goal, but they could not set out until the police hunt had died down. He would have to take the little girl with him; his grandmother would know how to find her mother and father. He didn't know what to do about the dog; he supposed it would have to come too. He quite liked it now.

In the potting-shed he found a sack containing a few old potatoes. They were rather green, but if he baked them they might be all right. He'd need to light a fire, though.

He found a half-empty book of matches on the damp grass by the drive where Mick Green had dropped it the night before.

CHAPTER
EIGHTEEN

With the discovery of the matches a fire became possible, and Jamie patiently assembled the ingredients. There was some coal in the shed, and he found an old pail with a hole in the bottom which he filled with small pieces. He carried some larger lumps up by hand and got very dirty doing it. But there was a rainwater butt, and he washed in that; doing so reminded him that he was thirsty. It wouldn't do to drink that water; there were insects in it. The pond water would be dirty too. He found an old jam jar, which he rinsed in the water butt and he tried all the taps in the house to collect any dregs. He understood what had happened — that the mains were turned off — for his father did this at home before they left for their annual holiday. But he could not see how to turn them on again; there were various wheels and taps in different places but nothing happened when he turned them, and one was too stiff to budge.

He put his jam jar on the ground in the open, to catch any rain that might fall in the night. Then he tried to light his fire.

First he crumpled some paper in the grate and arranged dry twigs above it, as his grandmother did; his own home was centrally heated with no open fire. Then he struck a match, but nothing happened. The dew had been heavy in the night and he had wasted several matches before he understood that they were damp; then he almost wept, but what would the little girl think if she woke and found him crying? Warmth might help, and he put the match-book, which now held only five unspent matches, inside his shirt against his body. Holding it in position with his arm across his chest like Napoleon, he went downstairs to the telephone. He'd decided to ring up his grandmother; she might come and collect them all. He thought with longing of her comfortable cottage and the chocolate cakes she made, which his mother deplored. He knew her number; he had rung her before; one of Lydia's tenets was that children should know whom to ring in emergency, apart from dialling 999.

But he could not get through. Several times that afternoon Jamie vainly tried the disconnected telephone. He didn't understand why it wasn't working, except that telephones did go out of order. If he kept on trying, it might be mended in the end.

Norman longed to see Felicity, but it wouldn't be right so soon; however, he could telephone. He dialled her number, but there was no reply.

Now that the police and Mrs Bowling had gone, it was very quiet. He couldn't just sit about the flat, alone.

He took the van and drove out to the country, where he went for a long walk and thought about the past; there was a lot to remember. He knew that there would be a period in which he must exist in a sort of limbo — mourn Emma, wait for the law to take its course and find whoever had so savagely killed her — and at last adjust to his new freedom.

When he got home he felt, suddenly, ravenously hungry. All at once he realized that there was no need, now, to exist on lean meat, salads and fruit; he could eat whatever took his fancy — suet dumplings, potato chips, pastries and cream. He washed and changed; then he went out again, got into the van, and drove to Muddington where he consumed a large and expensive meal at The Rose and Crown.

While he was out, Felicity, back from her Sunday outing, telephoned. She wanted to express some sort of horror and sympathy at what had happened, though she did not know quite how to do it. She was rather relieved when there was no reply. At least she had tried.

When Norman returned, replete, and warmed not only by the food but by a modest half-bottle of claret, he saw a car drawing up outside the shop. From it emerged the formidable thickset figure of Detective Inspector Cudlipp.

"I'd like a word, Mr Widnes," said Cudlipp, as Norman unlocked the door of the shop. "If you don't mind."

"At this time of night? Surely you know everything I can tell you already," said Norman.

"Just a point or two, as we've the chance," said the inspector. "Save me asking you to come round to the station in the morning."

"Oh, very well," said Norman.

He led the way upstairs to the flat, and sat down himself in the upright chair he had occupied earlier when making his statement. Detective Inspector Cudlipp remained standing.

"Your mother died very suddenly, Mr Widnes," he said, without preamble.

"My mother!" The apparent inconsequentiality of this remark took Norman by surprise. "Not at all. She'd been ill for years," he said.

"But in fact the end was sudden," the inspector insisted.

"No one ever knows what to expect in those cases," said Norman, but his palms had begun to sweat.

The inspector, standing in the middle of the room, suddenly seemed large and hostile. His pale blue eyes gazed steadily at Norman.

"Mr Widnes, there is sympathy for people who end the sufferings of very sick people, but it's still against the law," he said.

He couldn't know about the capsules. No one did, now.

"What are you suggesting?" Norman asked, speaking carefully.

"I'm not suggesting anything at present, Mr Widnes, I'm establishing facts. Very soon after your mother's death you married your late wife — a woman many years older than yourself."

"Is that forbidden?" demanded Norman, angry now.

"It's unusual," said the inspector. "Did you marry her, or did she marry you?"

Norman did not answer. Why should he tell this man that they had already been lovers for months?

"You were a young man with a good business — she was ageing," said Cudlipp. "You gave her security."

169

"It wasn't like that," said Norman. "You wouldn't understand."

"Mr Widnes, if you did help your mother on her way it would be difficult to prove it now," said Cudlipp.

"I didn't help her on her way, as you put it, and what has this to do with finding the devil who killed Emma?" Norman's voice was unsteady.

"Your wife would have known the truth about your mother's death." Cudlipp went on as if he had not spoken.

"If I'd killed my mother, as you seem to be suggesting, yes, my wife would have known, but I didn't," said Norman. Now he was really sweating. "I don't see what you're getting at."

But he did. What could have put the thought into the inspector's head?

Before Cudlipp could tell him, the telephone rang. Neither man moved, and after several rings Cudlipp said, "Well, aren't you going to answer it?"

As Norman had expected, it was Felicity. It was just the wrong moment for him to speak to her.

"Yes. Yes, terrible," he said into the instrument, and turned his back to the inspector. "Yes — I've been out." Pause, while he listened. Cudlipp studied the ceiling. "I know. I suppose they'll find him," Norman said. "The police are here now, as a matter of fact. Oh, I don't know. More questions." There was another pause, and he added, "No, not for a while. I'll let you know. Thank you for ringing," and he hung up.

"Who was that?" inquired Cudlipp as Norman came back to his seat.

170

"Just a friend," said Norman.

"Her name?"

"I don't see why I should tell you that, Inspector."

"But it was a woman?"

Norman had fallen straight into the inspector's trap.

"What's wrong with that?" he asked brusquely.

"I'm not suggesting that anything is. Is it?" The inspector's tone was mild but his pale eyes were like ice. "Well, if you won't tell me her name, I shall have to find out from someone else who your friends are, shan't I ?" he said, and on that note he left.

In the intervals of trying to telephone his grandmother, Jamie arranged his resources. The tea chest stood on its side in front of the grate, with the supplies inside it. Three bananas were left, and some bread, and there were lots of apples. He had found some sacks, which could he added to the curtains to act as blankets. Both he and Laura had thick clothes, and Jamie had now discovered that the dog, nestled against, gave out a comforting warmth.

Boris had whined and snuffled by the door for a while, and Jamie had grown nervous again.

"Lie down. Good dog," he had urged.

At last, resignedly, the dog had gone to a corner of the room and raised his leg, and Jamie, in a flood of shame, had understood. He had used the lavatory himself, and had sternly taken Laura there too, though in her case it was once again too late; it was the proper place, even though it would not flush.

He shared another banana with her, cuddling her on his knee, gave her some bread and some to the dog, and ate some himself. Then, since it was dark by now, he decided it was bedtime and settled all three of them down for the night. They huddled close to one another on the curtains with the sacks drawn over them as coverings.

Jamie fell asleep in the middle of telling Laura the story of the Three Bears, complete with different voices.

That evening Paula drank a great deal of gin and began to feel more and more ill-used. Harry had not been round since the night Guy had come home and she was beginning to think he would never return. Guy himself, who should have been in her bed, had stolen their child. She grew still more maudlin, until at last she decided to telephone Guy in London.

When he answered, she did not at first believe that he had not got Laura. It took Guy some time, too, to understand from her garbled tale that the child and the Labrador were missing. Then he said that he would come down at once, and told her to call the police.

In case she was incapable of doing so, he rang them himself before leaving. It was weeks since he had seen Laura, and he really did not know how far a child of her age could wander.

"You mean you went off for the day in the car thinking I'd got her?" he demanded, when he reached the house, and found Paula sprawled in a basket chair in the kitchen, with a half-empty gin bottle on the table. "You must be out of your mind."

Paula was dressed in a loose shirt, a long shaggy cardigan, tight jeans, and had rows of metal chains round her rather grubby neck. Surely she hadn't always looked like this? Guy regarded her with horrified distaste.

"You're not natural," he said.

"Is that what you think?" She laughed in his face. "You didn't once," and she opened her mouth at him, showing her tongue.

He slapped her face.

"Sober up, you bitch," he said.

Into this domestic scene came the police. A woman constable had already been to see Paula and obtained a description of the missing child. There was no photograph available, and she'd reported that the mother was too drunk to give a clear account of how the child had disappeared — she'd refused to have a policewoman left in the house with her, and seemed bent on getting still more drunk.

"What do you think has happened to Laura?" Guy asked the sergeant who now arrived. "It can't be connected with the murder, surely?"

"I agree that it's highly unlikely, but we can't rule it out," said the sergeant. "Now, Mr Curtis, your version of the events, please."

Guy described how he had heard of Laura's disappearance, not concealing his disgust at Paula's conduct. The sergeant noted the details down with an impassive expression, but the air vibrated with unspoken condemnation.

After the police car had driven away, Guy remembered that Laura had not been in her usual room when he was last at the house and he went to see where she had been sleeping. When he found her cot in the small ground-floor room and saw the state it was in, he was overcome with rage, shame, and his own guilt.

He came back into the kitchen where Paula still sat at the table, sprawling in her chair and fingering her necklaces. He caught hold of the back of her cardigan and jerked her to her feet.

"My God, I could kill you!" he said. "And you'd better keep out of my way or I probably will."

For a moment Paula's eyes flashed and a smile began on her none-too-clean face. Guy recognized the expression and flung her away from him.

"You're obscene," he said, and rushed out of the house. He got into his car and drove at high speed into the country where he stopped, lurched out on to the grass verge, and was violently sick.

After he had gone a reporter who was covering the story of Emma and who had followed the police to the house, rang the front-door bell. He was able to take a photograph of Paula before she slammed the door in his face. His wait outside had not been in vain; he had a scoop from the murder town for the morning papers.

"You were quite right, sir," said Cudlipp. "Widnes has got a woman. She rang him up and he wouldn't say who she was."

Detective Superintendent Beddoes had been drawing cylindrical doodles on his blotting pad while he listened to Cudlipp's account of his interview with Norman. "Someone will know who she is. He won't have managed to keep it a secret from everybody. Shouldn't be hard to find out," said Cudlipp. "That's where he went with the wine every week. He was on foot, so she must be local. He'd not enough time for anyone further afield."

The superintendent added fine shading to one of his columns.

"Do you think Widnes tried to kill his wife?" he asked. "Saw his chance after the break-in?"

"No, I don't, and for two reasons," said Cudlipp.

"Well?"

"First, he knew too much about illness to make such a mistake. He'd looked after his mother for years. He'd have seen that the woman was dead."

For by now the pathologist's report had shown that Emma had died seconds before the blow that shattered her skull.

"And second?"

"I doubt if he could be so brutal — and that's borne out by what Dr Barrett said about him — a kind man, and lacking in drive," said Cudlipp.

"He might have got carried away," hazarded the superintendent. "Lost his head — understandable, if he was in the grip of some great passion," he added fancifully, drawing a heart on the blotter, and an arrow to pierce it. N.W., he inscribed, and a question mark.

Cudlipp had been watching, from his upside-down view, these artistic forays.

"No, sir," he said. "I don't think so, but we could lean on him a bit and take it from there. Best be certain."

"Do that," said the superintendent. "And the thief? He's the one we really want."

"We haven't any line at all," Cudlipp admitted. "No prints. Just the girl's, Madge Pearce's, on the safe, and Widnes' too, of course."

"Widnes never used a night safe?"

"Couldn't rely on getting out to the bank. Had to stay with his missus. Hundreds of prints in the shop, of course, with the customers — no unexpected ones in the flat. Chummy was careful."

"And cool."

"Yes."

"What's Widnes' mood like now?" asked Beddoes.

"Better," said Cudlipp, and looked disapproving. "He'd been having a bloody great meal at The Rose and Crown. I checked. Ate right through the menu — wine and the lot."

"Like a celebration, eh?"

"You could look at it that way."

Beddoes scratched out the heart, leaving the initials and the query.

"Find the lady," he said.

176

CHAPTER
NINETEEN

Jamie woke when it began to grow light the next morning. As he stirred, Boris moved, stretched, and got up, tail wagging. Laura was still sleeping, so Jamie laid a finger to his lips as if the dog could understand the gesture and softly opened the door. The two went downstairs and Jamie let Boris out, watching while he sniffed about. Soon he came back and padded upstairs, waiting for Jamie to let him into the room where Laura was.

While he was standing on the back doorstep waiting for Boris, Jamie heard the whine of a milk float passing along the road and it gave him an idea. Shutting Boris in with Laura, he went down the drive and peered out into the road. The milk float had disappeared round the corner and there was no sign of the frightening Alsatian. Jamie ran along the road until he came to a doorstep with four pints of milk standing on it. He took one and turned to go; then he changed his mind and took a second: babies needed a lot of milk and he felt very thirsty himself.

He got back to the big upstairs room just as Laura woke and they had breakfast of milk and dry bread followed by a banana. He and Laura drank, taking turns, from one of the bottles, and then he held it for the dog to lap what was left, half trickling it into his mouth. Boris soon got the idea. Jamie was tempted to open the second bottle but decided to set it aside for later.

Then he tackled the fire. He suddenly felt very cold and Laura's hands were icy.

This time the first match struck, but the paper in the grate was damp and so was the chimney; it smoked furiously.

Jamie worked away at it, blowing from below as he had seen his grandmother do and feeding in tiny dry sticks which he had found in the shed. It caught, but only just, and continued to smoke. Now he must watch Laura and not leave her alone in the room with the fire. They would soon warm up.

Jamie began to talk to her, trying to teach her his name.

A massive police hunt for the two missing children began early that morning, and a constable patrolling a country district got out of his car to search the roadside ditches. He went through a gateway and into a field. There he found the body of Pedro. Because the dog's head was shattered he reported it instantly.

Despite her mother's protests Madge insisted on going to work, so Mrs Pearce sent the girl off with sandwiches as usual, and a hearty kiss which was not part of the normal routine.

"Come back if you're not needed," she said. "Or come round to the cleaner's. I can always find you something to do."

178

Before she left for work herself, she glanced at the newspaper. TERROR TOWN STRUCK AGAIN, she read, and beneath the banner headline saw a picture of the woman whose child had been wailing outside the cleaner's only the week before. It was a good photograph of Paula, and she recognized her instantly.

That old lady would know that it was the same woman too. She might have done the kiddy in — with someone like that, there was no telling. It would be easy to find out who the old lady was; Mrs Pearce distinctly remembered the skirt she had brought in, a hairy tweed, purplish and threadbare. Both of them might be needed as witnesses to what they'd seen. The Pearces were not on the telephone, but Edna wasted no time.

It was Kenneth Armitage who saw the smoke. He was taking Gyp for a run to the corner of Foster Avenue, before breakfast, and he noticed it issuing from the chimney of what he thought was an empty house. At first he supposed that new owners had moved in without his knowledge but when he walked on to look there was no sign of an occupant and the "For Sale" board was still in position. He walked up the path and looked through the downstairs windows. There was no fire visible in any of the grates.

A respectable citizen and councillor, Kenneth rang the police and, to be on the safe side, the fire brigade.

The hardware shop was open. Norman was tidying the stock after the going-over the police had given it. It was business as usual. But there were no customers.

Madge did not know what to say about the tragedy, but no words were needed. Norman just said that Emma had been fond of her and added that they wouldn't talk about what had happened as it was too dreadful to discuss and the police were getting on with finding out who was responsible.

Outside in the square two workmen arranged barriers round a manhole cover, took it off, put up a little tin hut and disappeared inside to drink tea. They were two plain-clothes men who were watching the shop to see what women customers Norman had and if he seemed over-friendly with any of them.

Later, Mrs Bowling arrived, with ingredients for a hot-pot since calories need no longer be counted; she made a baked custard too. She and Norman ate it together while Madge as usual sat in the store with her sandwiches.

"We ought to ask her up," said Norman. "There's plenty for her." He wasn't hungry today.

"If you once start that, you'll have to keep on," said Mrs Bowling. "Leave it. Take my tip, it's for the best. She's very upset too — better keep her out of this room for a bit — it's so quiet. She'd feel it."

It was quiet. It was strange to have no Emma lying there, ponderous, on the sofa.

"You'll be making some changes," Mrs Bowling stated.

"I suppose I will," said Norman. "Not yet, though. We'll carry on the same for the present, if that suits you."

Mrs Bowling agreed. She could hardly believe that there would be no more smuggled swiss rolls and éclairs; no romances to collect from the library; no Thursday evening card games.

"When's the funeral to be?" she asked.

Norman shrugged.

"We can't arrange anything till after the inquest," he said. "That will probably be on Wednesday, I've been told."

Emma would be cremated. Norman wanted no memorial tombstone. As far as was possible, everything must be expunged, as when his mother died, though nothing could obliterate memories; they could haunt for ever.

After lunch Mrs Minter came into the shop and found Madge realigning packs of clothes pegs on a shelf.

"I'm not here to buy anything," said Mrs Minter. "I came to express my sympathy to Mr Widnes. Is he about?"

Madge fetched him from the store-room. He was grateful to Mrs Minter for calling.

"We might as well be closed," he said. "No one's come in all day."

Mrs Minter had noticed this. She was rather surprised. She had expected a flood of the curious, but instead they had flocked to the other shops in the square and stood staring over at Widnes' Stores. The two men in the hut over the manhole had been obliged to produce some tools and climb down — or one had climbed down, while his companion kept an eye on what was happening.

"There will be some customers now," Mrs Minter prophesied. She had heard the onlookers discussing what to do; some thought Norman heartless to open after what had happened, but others admired him for it and there was a lot of sympathy for him.

Mrs Minter was right. When she left, a stream of customers flowed in; some had clearly come to gape at Norman and study the scene of the crime but many more mumbled a few words of condolence. The two detectives outside left their work and sauntered across, talking to one another as they watched who came and went. They noticed Felicity's Fiat slow down while she looked at the shop. Then she parked and got out. When she went inside and began talking to Norman, one of them followed.

To Felicity, Norman looked much as usual; perhaps a little paler. He told her he did not know how the hunt for the killer was getting on.

"Well, at least the lost children have turned up," Felicity said.

Norman had forgotten all about Jamie. He had never known about Laura's disappearance.

"Two children? Jamie Renshaw —" He did not finish the sentence.

"Another child vanished too — wandered off. They turned up in that empty house in Foster Avenue. They're quite all right. I don't know how the two of them got together — some prank of Jamie's, I think."

Norman thought vaguely that Jamie wasn't the sort of child to go in for pranks, but he had too much on his mind to worry about that.

"I'll ring you when I can," he said to Felicity.

She wanted to reply that she was rather busy, but she couldn't do it.

The detective who had entered the shop behind her could not hear the conversation, but the earnest manner

182

of it and the fact that she bought nothing was significant. He bought a torch battery himself, from Madge. Then he left the shop and nodded to his colleague. In a few seconds information about Felicity and the number of her car were being radioed to their headquarters.

Both the police and the fire brigade had converged on the empty house that morning, after Kenneth's telephone call.

The police wasted no time banging on the door. They broke in, not knowing what to expect inside. Upstairs, they found one of the bedroom doors locked, for Jamie, hearing them, had turned the key. He crouched in a corner of the room his arm round Laura who had began to cry. The fire which had betrayed their presence smouldered smokily, but the room was still very cold, and although he was frightened to the core of his being, a sense of relief swamped Jamie too.

"Open up. Police," said the sergeant who had arrived. He did not really expect whoever had bashed Emma Widnes on the head to be lurking inside; chummy wouldn't give himself away by lighting a fire when he had been so careful about fingerprints, but he had a brief fantasy, nevertheless, of finding an adult villain inside the room. Laura's wailing upset this idea, but it was the firemen with their ladder to the window who in fact discovered the identity of the fugitives. It did not take them very long to persuade Jamie to open the door.

By the time Mrs Pearce called at the police station on Monday morning Laura had already been found, but a constable took down the details of the incident at the cleaners. A customer had seen it too, Mrs Pearce added: Mrs Costello of Old Bidbury; she had checked the name on the cleaning ticket.

That evening, since she and Harry were now on good terms until he went off chasing some new woman, she told him about it.

Listening to the story, Harry was sickened. It was a nasty business and he was well out of it. He'd better keep his trap shut, too, or he'd find himself involved in a baby battering case. He was appalled to think that the child, whom he'd never seen, had been lying in that state while he was in the house. He'd heard her crying as he left for the last time, but until then he'd barely been aware of her existence.

In future he'd be more careful.

After a night of anxiety such as she had never before known in her well-planned life, relief made Lydia loquacious. When she knew that Jamie was safe she poured out to the police the whole story of his fear of the Alsatian, his walks to school with Norman Widnes and his father's rebuke to Norman.

The inference was clear, and the report was passed on to Detective Inspector Cudlipp.

"It throws new light on Widnes," he said to the superintendent.

"You mean he's a kinky character fond of little boys?" asked the superintendent. "Didn't strike me that way, I must say."

"Nor me," said Cudlipp. "I still can't get over him going out the night after his wife died and gorging himself at The Rose and Crown."

"A man must eat, and a decent dinner isn't exactly gorging," remarked Beddoes. "I think you'll find there's a discreet widow somewhere in the background, or maybe a divorcée — that's what he'd go for."

"We'll soon know," said Cudlipp. "Nothing's been reported from the shop yet. If there is someone, and she doesn't go to see him, in the end he'll contact her. We've only to wait."

"Nasty business about that little girl," said Beddoes.

"Lucky for her she met up with young Jamie Renshaw," said Cudlipp. "He took good care of her, it seems. Unlike her mother."

"Parents," sighed Beddoes, who had one wayward daughter whom he idolized. "Some don't care, and some care too much, eh?"

"Right, sir," said Cudlipp, who laid down strict rules for his own family's conduct and was so far obeyed. "Someone had stashed a motor-bike in the bushes at that house where the children were found," he went on. "It was recent — it could have been Saturday — it hasn't rained since then and the tyre marks were pretty distinct. It was in a sheltered spot under some bushes. Wouldn't have been seen from the road. Might have some bearing. There was a fag end there too, and a spent match."

The constable who had earlier searched the grounds of the house and tried its doors while the children were inside had atoned for his failure to find them by showing extra zeal when sent to the scene later, and had made these discoveries.

"Well, that's a line anyway, wherever it leads," said Beddoes.

"It's all we've got," said Cudlipp.

After they were found, both Jamie and Laura were taken to hospital, but Jamie was allowed to go home, where he was given a bath and put to bed. The police had extracted a somewhat confused account from him of what had happened. It was certain that he had had no contact with anyone, apart from Laura, and that Paula's treatment of Laura was the only offence in law committed against the children.

Geoffrey spent some time talking to the policewoman to whom Jamie had told his tale. That afternoon he went to see Sarah. She was in the kitchen eating a chocolate biscuit while Simon gnawed a rusk.

"Have some tea," she said. "And a biscuit. Sorry about the muddle."

She had been ironing, and a pile of shirts was stacked on the ironing board.

"Isn't Kenneth drip-dry?" asked Geoffrey. Lydia did very little ironing.

"No."

"You should convert him," said Geoffrey, and added, "I'd love a biscuit. Thanks."

"I'm so thankful about Jamie," Sarah said. "It's been awful."

"Poor little blighter — he's upset about some milk he stole off a doorstep. Thinks he'll be sent to prison for it," said Geoffrey. "I feel terrible about the whole thing, Sarah. Bloody guilty. It might all have ended very differently."

"Well, it didn't," said Sarah.

"It was all my fault," Geoffrey told her, bent on purging himself. "It seems he didn't want to go to the safari park and he doesn't want a dog. We'd decided to give him one, you see, to cure him of his phobia. He heard us talking. The police got all this out of him. Awful to think your child will talk to a policewoman and not to you."

"Well he is cured, isn't he?" Sarah said. "That Labrador was with them all the time. He was very sensible, Geoffrey. You should be proud of him. He kept that other child warm and safe, and fed her too, even if he did pinch the milk. He showed lots of initiative. He looked after the poor little thing better than her own mother did, from what I've heard."

"That's true," said Geoffrey. "Can I have another biscuit?"

Sarah pushed the tin across to him. She thought fleetingly that she and Kenneth never had tea cosily like this together; it had to be cups and saucers and plates, preferably in the sitting-room, never mugs and fingers in the kitchen.

"I suppose every man wants his son to be brave," Geoffrey said, taking two biscuits out of the tin.

"Are you brave?" Sarah asked him.

"No I'm not," said Geoffrey. "That's why I want Jamie to be — I don't want him to be a weak, craven individual."

"He's not weak or craven — he's already proved that," Sarah said. "If a person's never afraid, they've nothing to be brave about. Jamie must have needed plenty of courage to hang on to that Labrador and not run screaming home, even if the whole business was a misguided affair."

"He fished the child out of the pond," Geoffrey said. "From what he said, I think the dog may have been trying to haul her out too — it seems he had hold of her anorak. But he was rather confused. We'll understand more when he's had a sleep and can talk about it again."

"You must make him understand you're not angry," Sarah said earnestly. "I think you should let him see you think he acted bravely, even though you were worried to bits."

"You're right about that," said Geoffrey. "And you think we shouldn't get a dog?"

"I do. Maybe a rabbit or a hamster — but only if he wants one. Geoff, some people don't like animals all that much and are still perfectly nice. People are more important than pets, though you wouldn't think so sometimes from the fuss that's made about animals."

"Lydia thinks if you don't relate to animals, you're missing a basic human experience," said Geoffrey.

"Maybe you make up for it some other way," said Sarah. "Look at Mrs Minter — she can't stand all the dogs there are around here but she's a perfectly normal person. I admire her, too, battling on by herself without even a canary for company. She must often be lonely."

"You've got Gyp," Geoffrey stated, and he thought, you're lonely too.

"Yes. He's company, but I don't treat him as a lap-dog," said Sarah. "Simon can't say much for himself yet, can you, poppet?" and she wiped his messy chin with his bib.

Geoffrey reflected that Gyp's conversational powers were strictly limited too, but no more than Kenneth's, probably. He wanted to laugh at this thought, and to share it, but obviously he couldn't with Sarah. What on earth could she see in that pompous oaf, he wondered, and then realized that it wasn't funny at all.

"I'll get Jamie a bike," he said aloud. "Then if that Alsatian's still around, he can pedal past, pretty quick. I'll teach him to ride safely."

"The police run road safety courses, I believe," said Sarah helpfully, pleased with this idea.

"Yes, I think they do," said Geoffrey, and added, "I wish I hadn't bawled poor Widnes out about meeting Jamie. He was being extremely kind, really. I feel pretty ashamed about it now."

Sarah played with the sugar, digging into it with a spoon.

"You thought you were doing the right thing for your child," she excused. "At least you're able to admit to making a mistake." Kenneth would never admit to a fault.

"Jamie likes you," Geoffrey said. "I think you understand him better than Lydia or I do."

"I'm fond of him," said Sarah.

They were silent. Between them unspoken, hung all sorts of confessions and avowals.

"You'll move away," said Sarah at last. "Lydia wants to, doesn't she?"

"Yes. But it won't happen yet."

"You'll go up in the world. That's Ken's aim too. It's all he thinks about," said Sarah. "He's going to take up bridge next. He thinks it's useful. I've refused."

"Lydia plays," said Geoffrey. "I don't."

There was another silence. Sarah piled up hills of sugar and then demolished them.

"That little girl — Laura — what will happen to her?" she asked.

"I should think she'll be taken into care. She's safe at the moment, in hospital. Curtis nearly tore his wife apart, it seems, when he found out the state the kid was in."

"He'd have known about it if he'd come home more often."

"That's true."

"She's doomed really, isn't she? That child? One of them will get her and neither of them really wants her."

"The father may do something about it. Who knows?"

"You never do know, really, do you, what's going on between people?" Sarah said.

Geoffrey took her hand.

"Sometimes you do," he said.

Soon after half-past five that afternoon, Detective Inspector Cudlipp and Detective Sergeant French arrived at Widnes' Stores. Madge had just left, and as she waited for the bus she saw them enter the shop. They must know the truth about what had happened by now; Mick would implicate her and Norman would never speak to her again: this last reflection loomed larger than any other.

Norman, meanwhile, had taken the policemen up to the flat. The sitting-room smelled of polish, for Mrs Bowling had given it a good going over, and it had an antiseptic, impersonal aura. The sofa over by the window still dominated the room, as it had when occupied by Emma. Her mohair rug, neatly folded, lay on the seat.

"You were in the habit of meeting young Jamie Renshaw every morning and taking him to school," began the inspector in a tougher tone than he had used even the night before.

"Just recently, yes," said Norman. This had nothing to do with Emma.

"Why was that?"

"I discovered that he was often late for school. He was afraid of Mrs Curtis's Alsatian — it always stands in the road — and he avoided it by coming round this way. I took him past." Even to himself, Norman's explanation sounded defensive.

"You didn't tell his parents?"

"I meant to, but I hadn't really had time," said Norman. "I spoke to Mrs Curtis, but it made no difference."

"Curious that you could find time to take the boy along the road, yet not inform his parents."

"I would have, when I'd time," said Norman. "I'm sorry I didn't. The boy mightn't have gone missing if his parents had realized."

"You could have telephoned."

Norman looked surprised.

"I didn't think of that — I could have done, I suppose. It just seemed to need the personal touch."

"Mr Renshaw discovered what had been happening and asked you to stop, however."

"Yes." Norman still smarted at the memory.

"Why did you think he did this, Mr Widnes?"

"Ask him," retorted Norman.

Cudlipp judged that the moment had come to put on some pressure. He fixed upon Norman his icy-blue stare.

"Mr Widnes, having an invalid wife was a great tie," he said.

"Yes. But other men have sick wives," said Norman.

"You're free now, however, to enjoy — shall we call it a wider social life?"

"I haven't thought about it," Norman said.

"You might marry again, for instance."

"That's an indecent suggestion," Norman said angrily. "My wife was brutally killed only two days ago."

But he had admitted the same thought to himself only hours after Emma's death: he need not lose Felicity.

Cudlipp was continuing.

"Mr Widnes, when you got back on Saturday night and found the place had been robbed, was your wife already dead?"

"Of course she was. You saw her. Those dreadful injuries — thank God at least she must have died at once."

"You didn't seize the chance to get rid of her, throwing the blame on the thief? She wasn't just lying there shocked — unconscious, perhaps — after the robbery and you finished her off?"

Norman's face reddened with fury.

"Inspector, I loved my wife," he said. "I would never have hurt her. What you're saying is horrible. Besides,

192

aren't you forgetting that you found the safe in the garden?"

"You could have put it there," said Cudlipp.

Norman's guilt about Felicity had already made him evasive, but he had never foreseen the nightmare accusation. He felt trapped.

"Where did you go on Saturday night after you left The Grapes?" Cudlipp asked.

"I've already told you. I went for a walk. I often do. I often used to leave Emma for an hour or two — she liked me to go out. She had the telephone beside her. She could ring up Mrs Bowling in an emergency, or the doctor."

"No one's come forward to say that they saw you that night," said Cudlipp.

"Why should they? It was dark — I don't suppose anyone noticed me. Inspector, a criminal killed my wife — some evil thug — why aren't you looking for him?"

"We are, Mr Widnes, we are," said Cudlipp, and now he spoke in a softer voice. "I believe you are acquainted with Miss Felicity Baxter?"

Madge got off the bus and walked up the road towards her home, her mind still with Norman. What had he learned from the police, she wondered dismally. She was sure that Mick would somehow put all the blame on her — and it was her fault, after all. But what else could she have done?

She should have told Norman what had happened. But she hadn't, and now it was too late. Even so, she could have confessed today about her part in the affair; he was so good that he might somehow manage to forgive her. But it had all been so dreadful that she could never talk about it to anyone.

Her thoughts went miserably round in her mind while she trudged on and turned into the quiet road where she lived. Suddenly there was a roar behind her as a motor-bike, driven fast, sped towards her. Madge felt a blow in her back; then she was thrown into the air, pitching on to her head against the kerb.

After the two policemen had gone, Norman sat staring at the wall in a state of dulled incredulity. His anger had all gone, faced with the fantastic allegation that he had murdered Emma.

The police knew about Felicity, and to them it was excuse enough. And there had been times when he had longed for freedom: days and nights when the thought of ministering to that gross body filled him with repugnance: moments when he longed for the chance to live without having to think of her before anything else. Then he would remind himself of the secret they shared, and of the heavy cost of silence.

CHAPTER
TWENTY

The police had soon traced Felicity by means of her car registration number and on a map of the area they discovered how easy it was to reach her flat from Norman's shop; the journey on foot across the fields would take less than ten minutes.

After they left Norman, Cudlipp and French went to see her. At first she thought they had come about Jamie Renshaw, and when they asked her if she knew Norman her surprise was genuine. But she answered at once.

"Everyone knows him," she said. "Everyone uses his shop."

"You called there this afternoon without buying anything," said Cudlipp.

Felicity hesitated. Should she say he was out of whatever she had gone to buy? She did not want to be involved with Norman in his trouble, but her planned walking away from him could not be as coldly calculated as to deny him altogether; besides, she was not naturally a liar.

"I called to offer my sympathy," she said. "It was a terrible thing to happen."

"What do you know about the death of Mr Widnes' mother?" Cudlipp asked.

"His mother?" Felicity's astonishment at this question showed in her voice. "Not much," she said. "It happened before I came, here. Why?"

"You've heard no gossip? No suggestion that she was helped on her way?"

"Never! What a monstrous idea!"

"What's your assessment of Mr Widnes?" Cudlipp continued unruffled.

"My assessment? Why should I think about him at all?" Felicity demanded. "I thought you'd come here to talk about my pupil, Jamie Renshaw."

"No. That's a separate matter," said Cudlipp. "Although Mr Widnes had been escorting him to school every morning for at least a week. You knew that, didn't you?"

"Why should I?" Felicity parried, but her heart sank. The police must have found out somehow about her and Norman; it was the only explanation for their presence, and exposure could only bring trouble.

"You'll be seeing more of him, now that he's free," Cudlipp stated.

His unblinking stare made Felicity feel uncomfortable, but she answered at once.

"Certainly not. It's got nothing to do with me. And anyway, I'm leaving Bidbury. I've applied for post in Canada."

"There's our motive," said Cudlipp, as he and French left. "She was chucking him and moving on."

"We've got to prove they were having an affair. It may not be easy," said French, who thought Felicity seemed an iron-willed young woman from whom it would be difficult to get any sort of admission.

"We'll soon find someone who saw them together," Cudlipp said. "Just slip back, meanwhile, and look in her dustbin. You might find an empty wine bottle in it. With prints."

Mick was away from the scene of Madge's accident in seconds, before anyone else arrived. It was lucky she lived in such a quiet street, he thought, zooming off in a cloud of exhaust. He left her lying in a huddle on the pavement; she'd be silent now, all right, and for a good long time, he hoped. Even for keeps.

He had been startled when his mother said she had come to see him. It had to be Madge, from the description. And it tied in with her asking Reg where he lived.

"What a nerve," he'd said.

"Not your usual sort, I'd say," his mother remarked, primming her lips.

"Fancies me, she does," said Mick. "But I'm not interested — get it? In case she comes again."

He couldn't think what she had in mind; not shopping him, for sure; she'd never have come to see him if that was it. The reason he'd given his mother must be the right one.

All the same, it was only sense to leave nothing to chance.

Felicity risked telephoning Norman. He must be warned.

"The police came to ask if I knew you," she said. "I didn't tell them anything, but somehow they suspect."

"Does it matter?" Norman asked wearily. He had denied their allegations, but he knew that Cudlipp was not deceived. "Once this is all over, Felicity —"

"I'll be gone, Norman," Felicity said. "I've told you already. I'm leaving Bidbury."

"But things are different now —"

"No. Sorry. I'm fond of you, Norman, and we've had some good times — but it's over now." She felt shame at what she was doing, but the sooner the break came after what had just happened, the better. "I'm sorry," she said again. She did not want to spend the rest of her life with Norman, and she did not want to see him alone again.

Norman hung up, not answering. There was nothing to say. Neither of them knew that a newspaper reporter had seen the police enter Felicity's flat.

"What about this, then?"

Detective Sergeant French came into Cudlipp's office on Tuesday morning holding by one corner, gingerly, so that any prints would not be smudged, a sheet of writing paper. Printed in large capitals, Madge's succinct message read:

MICK GREEN DID IT.

"Did what?" asked Cudlipp.

"Well, sir, the envelope was postmarked Bidbury," said French.

"Mick Green. Do we know a Mick Green?"

"Not yet."

"Better see if we can find one, then. And check for prints. Might give us something."

"Right, sir."

French went off to order the routine inquiries which would unearth any local Mick Greens. It was an ordinary sort of name and there might be several. It would all take time, and might in the end prove irrelevant, but that was what got results: the painstaking weaving together of different strands to build up a case. There was just the chance that prints on the letter might match up with those of someone already involved in the attack on Emma Widnes.

There were other letters, too, which had to be investigated, mostly from cranks, but all must be checked.

Meanwhile, Madge lay unconscious in hospital.

The van which Mick had used for the removal of Pedro had been found dumped in a back street in Muddington. Before its owner reclaimed it, the constable making the report on its recovery observed some pale dog hairs in it. He made a note of the fact, but otherwise thought it of no importance.

Another constable, on Tuesday morning, called to tell Mrs Costello about finding the dead dog. Because it wore no collar, and she knew Pedro had been wearing his when he disappeared, she wouldn't believe it was Pedro. He would never wander so far, she insisted, and demanded to see the body.

There was no more doubt then.

There were five Michael Greens easily traced in the Bidbury area, and more in Muddington. Probably there were others not recorded as resident — below voting age, newly arrived, not owners of motor vehicles. Slowly the work of checking them went on.

Meanwhile the wine bottle found in Felicity's dustbin showed Norman's fingerprints. There were others on it too — probably hers, and those of the publican who sold it. Detective Superintendent Beddoes swung to the belief that Norman, returning from his clandestine tryst, had found the place done over and had seized his chance. Cudlipp still maintained that he could not be so vicious, although a circumstantial case against him was developing. The best way to oppose it was to find the thief. Robbery on its own was one thing; robbery with violence was a very different matter.

"That tip-off letter — I wonder who wrote that," Beddoes mused.

"We'll soon know, sir," Cudlipp said. "Might be an accomplice of the thief who doesn't want to be an accessory to murder, but who's too scared to shop him properly."

They both remembered Madge's prints on the safe together, and both dismissed the thought that she could be concerned so that it was a surprise when they learned that hers, and only hers, were on the sheet of notepaper.

CHAPTER
TWENTY-ONE

When Harry Pearce learned that Paula Curtis had been a customer of Edna's, and that moreover Edna was prepared to testify that she had seen her maltreating the little girl, his unease grew. Paula would discover that he was Edna's husband and the truth about their affair might come out. Edna, at the least, was sure to cut up rough and it could all be very unpleasant.

It seemed like a judgement on his conduct when the police arrived to break the news of Madge's accident. United in anxiety about their daughter, Edna and Harry sat by her hospital bed as she lay bandaged and still semiconscious. She had no recollection, so far, of what had happened or how she had been struck down.

"She may remember later," said a nurse.

In another ward of the same hospital, Guy Curtis stood beside a high cot and looked down at the small human that was his daughter. She lay inert, but awake, staring at him apprehensively, quite silent. The ward sister, from whom came an almost visible aura of hostility, stood beside him.

"Malnutrition," she said. "Bruising on her body. Chafed skin from wet knickers. This apathy is the result of near starvation."

Guy felt horrified pity for the plight of the child but she stirred no magic chord of affection in him; yet he was responsible for her existence.

"I didn't know," he said. "What will happen now?"

"She'll be here for some time," said the sister with satisfaction.

"And then?"

"I expect the police will have something to say about the state she was in. It's to be hoped she'll be put into care."

What could he do about it? He couldn't look after her himself, roving about the world as he did, he thought, with relief. She would be better off with a foster parent than with him.

"I'll come and see her again," he said. "Perhaps she'll remember me then."

But he saw no reason why she should.

No one thought of telling Norman about Madge's accident until halfway through Tuesday morning, when her mother telephoned.

Things were still quiet in the shop. Norman knew from experience that people found it difficult to behave naturally towards the bereaved. This time, because of the circumstances, the effect seemed to be even greater; the few customers who did call were reluctant to look him in the eye.

If he had had time to read the newspaper, he would have understood that there was another cause besides mere diffidence. A reporter who had met Mrs Costello standing in Bodger's Self-Service in front of the pet foods and grieving because she no longer needed Meatimix, had recognized a likely source of gossip. As a consequence of the chat he had with her, he had written a piece suggesting that someone other than the thief could have killed Emma, and adding that Norman's mother had died very suddenly five years before. There was no mention of his mother's illness nor of any names, and the piece was very carefully worded so that it was not libellous, but the inference was there.

When the shop closed, Norman went to the hospital to see Madge. She woke to find him sitting by her bed, and it was like a dream, until she remembered about Emma.

"Oh, Mr Widnes," she mumbled. "I'm ever so sorry."

Norman patted her hand, thinking she was apologizing for absence from work.

"Don't worry, Madge," he said. "Just you get better." He was so used to sick women that he was not upset at being in a hospital ward among a row of them, only distressed by her misfortune. "What happened?" he asked.

"I don't know. I was walking along, and that's all I remember," she frowned. "Then, next thing, I was here."

"You don't know what hit you?"

"No — at least —" She hesitated. "I thought it must have been a car, but now I remember a noise." She concentrated hard. "It was a motor-bike," she said.

Norman thought that when he saw the police again he would mention this; he would not seek them out, however. On his way home, he went into The Grapes, where he had a beer and a grilled steak in the bar. No one seemed to want to talk to him and in fact several backs were turned. Even the landlord's manner was cool.

An evening paper lay on the bench seat near him and Norman glanced at it as he ate. On the centre page there was a picture of a very angry-looking Felicity. The caption below read: *Miss Felicity Baxter, 27, friend of ironmonger Norman Widnes whose invalid wife was brutally attacked after a robbery on Saturday night. Mr Widnes had left his wife alone and found her dead body after spending the evening out. Miss Baxter was photographed outside Old Bidbury Primary School where she is a teacher. She refused to talk to our reporter.*

It was vicious: deadly. Felicity's headmaster had been very angry when he saw the item earlier. And so was Norman now.

Mrs Pearce saw the paper too, and showed it to her son while they had their tea. The news of Madge was a little better, and the family was easier, with time to think of other things.

"Well, poor sod, I'm not surprised. Are you?" said Reg. "Stands to reason, doesn't it, married to that old bag."

"He always seemed so nice," said Edna Pearce. "He was ever so good to Madge. Who would have believed it?"

Reg said that in Norman's shoes he'd have found someone with a bit more spark to her than that teacher looked to have, though beggars couldn't be choosers, of course.

All men were the same, thought Edna bitterly, wanting their bread buttered on both sides. She went to see Madge in hospital that evening, arriving just after Norman had gone. Madge mentioned hearing a motor-

204

bike behind her just before the accident, but what with one thing and another, Mrs Pearce did not pass the information on to the police until the next day.

Detective Sergeant French had been looking through the station reports. A lost dog had been found with its head smashed; it had belonged to Mrs Costello from Old Bidbury over whose garden the intruder had gone on Saturday night. A stolen van found abandoned in Muddington had dog hairs in it: blond ones. The van had now been returned to its owners.

He reported the facts to Detective Inspector Cudlipp who ordered the van to be brought in again. The hairs could be matched with the corpse of the dog, if it had not yet been disposed of, and if the van had not been cleaned. Even if it had, traces might linger. There would be plenty of dog hairs to be found in Mrs Costello's cottage, to provide a match. There might even be prints in the van, with a bit of luck.

"And see if anyone saw a motor-bike entering the garden of that empty house on Saturday night," Cudlipp added. "One did, to make those tyre marks. Probably no connection — a courting couple or some such — but we must check it out."

French already had the matter in hand.

Various Michael Greens had been traced, ranging from a dentist to a retired pawnbroker. None seemed a likely candidate for the role of Emma's attacker, but now that Madge's fingerprints had been found on the letter, a policewoman was at the hospital waiting to take a statement.

Madge, however, could not talk; she had lapsed back again into unconsciousness, away from her problems.

By Wednesday morning the right Mick Green had still not been found. He was not on the electoral roll, and the police had only just started to check motor-cycle registrations.

Incensed by the newspapers' scandalmongering but nevertheless titillated by the revelation of Norman's acquaintance with Felicity, Mrs Bowling advised him to shut the shop until it had all blown over. People would soon forget, she said; what he needed was a holiday. Things fitted together in her mind now — little remarks of a sad nature that Emma had sometimes made and Mrs Bowling had not understood.

"I can't go away until the police have found whoever did it, Ivy," Norman said.

And what would be the point, anyway, without a companion? He missed Emma: it was strange not to hear her raucous laugh, see her small pig eyes disappearing into the fat folds of her face as she rocked back and forth at some joke or other. He even missed her for physical contact.

"You don't think I did it, then?" he asked Mrs Bowling.

"As if you could — I'd like to know who gave them that wicked idea," said Mrs Bowling angrily. "Not anyone who'd seen you with her — with either of them."

Norman remembered the capsules: a whole heap of them, carefully saved and emptied, their powder content administered in one mammoth dose. What would Mrs Bowling think if she knew the truth about that? But no one would ever know, now.

206

Mrs Bowling went with him to the inquest, sitting next to him in court with a proprietorial air, ready to defend him if need be from any attack. All the same, she could not help reflecting, it was strange about that Felicity Baxter; it must be true, or he'd be up in arms about it. He'd kept that dark; he might have kept other things dark, too.

The inquest was opened and adjourned after establishing simply the dead woman's identity. Detective Superintendent Beddoes, with the consent of the coroner, had decided not to reveal the actual cause of death and that it was not in fact a case of murder for the moment. The intent had been there; a would-be killer must be caught.

Detective Sergeant French was a painstaking officer. He had caused casts to be made of the tyre marks in the bushes at the empty house very promptly, in case rain were to wash them away, and a watch was kept to trace motor-cycles which they matched. There were a great many, but it was just possible that the right one might still yield traces of earth from the ground where it had been left. Meanwhile, the search for Mick Green produced one who owned a motor-cycle and lived in a block of flats in New Bidbury.

French went there, with a constable.

Mick was at work, said his mother, who had just returned from her shift at the supermarket, when they knocked at the door. And she did not know where he'd been on Saturday night, she added when asked. He always went out with a crowd, she said, but she never asked where. Yes, he did smoke.

She was not alarmed by the visit; she did not connect it with what had happened at Old Bidbury, although into her mind flicked the memory of Mick as a small boy, thumping his sister's head against a wall as he held her by the hair, because she'd refused to give him some sweets she'd bought. He might have been doing some petty thieving, she thought; he'd got a transistor radio that way, she knew, and one or two other things.

French found out from her where Mick worked. When he got back to the police station and learned that Madge Pearce remembered hearing a motor-bike approaching just before she was knocked down, as reported a few minutes before by her mother, the matter became much more urgent.

"We've got to get hold of that bike, sir," he told Cudlipp. "That girl may have been knocked down on purpose."

Cudlipp felt relieved. He didn't like the way things were shaping for Norman.

"Bring Mick Green in," he said.

That evening a white-faced Edna Pearce was waiting for Reg when he got home. The police had been to question her about her daughter's possible friendship with a Mick Green who was helping them with their inquiries into the break-in at Widnes' Stores.

"Has Mick been seeing our Madge — apart from that night when he brought her home?" she asked Reg.

"Mick and our Madge — not likely," said Reg, but his expression was wary. Madge had wanted to know Mick's address, after all; they could have been meeting. "Why?" he asked.

His mother told him.

Reg was shocked, and he did not attempt to bluff his way out of it. He hadn't seen Mick leaving work that day; usually they rode home at much the same time, but he'd been transferred to a different part of the factory recently and he'd thought nothing of it. Surely if Mick were guilty he'd not have stayed around waiting to get picked up? He told his mother that Mick had talked about robbing Widnes' Stores.

"But it was just fooling," he added. "Madge couldn't have had anything to do with it, even if Mick did do the job. But he'd never —" His voice trailed off as he realized just how grave a crime had been committed. Mick would: he was violent: Reg had seen him almost beat the daylights out of a little kid who'd been cheeky one day; the other lads had pulled him off the boy before he'd done him too much damage. He'd forgotten it till now.

"Madge hadn't been herself for a while, before this happened," Edna said.

Reg knew that this was true.

"But how could she have helped him? She didn't go out that night, did she?"

"I don't think so. But she could have — your dad and I were out ourselves," she said.

"She might have got him a key or something," Reg muttered, and then, "but she wouldn't, would she? She'd not be so stupid."

"The thief knew where to find the money," Edna said quietly. "Madge might have told him."

CHAPTER
TWENTY-TWO

Above the noise of the factory machines, Mick never heard the two policemen approach. He'd been thinking that he could give this lot up now — move off, go abroad, maybe, like on the TV ads, and lounge under a palm tree somewhere sunny till the money ran out and the fuss over the job had died down Then, suddenly, there was a solid male body on either side of him, a voice in his ear, and he was being walked quietly away and out into a car before he had time to protest He shouted a bit then, and when he got to the station he had plenty to say once the questions began. He'd been with a girl on Saturday night, and he gave her name.

He'd made certain she'd support his alibi, so he wasn't really worried. He, Mick Green, was above the law and untouchable.

When the police showed the girl a photograph of Mick and asked her about him, she confirmed what he said; unfortunately for Mick, when the police called her younger sister was at home, and she, too, recognised the photograph. She was one of the girls before whom Mick had been unable to resist flaunting himself outside the ironmonger's shop on Saturday evening before he hid the motor-bike at the empty house. The younger girl was certain and in the end her sister admitted that she might have made a mistake about what time she met Mick.

The police found Pedro's collar in Mick's room, along with several pairs of bikini briefs, an imitation pistol, a varied collection of keys, and some other souvenirs. And a lot of money.

"Well," Elsie said to Felicity in the staff-room. "I suppose it's true?" Her tone was sardonic.

"What is?" Felicity glared at her.

"That you'd been having an affair with the ironmonger."

Felicity thought of denying it, but what was the point? No one would believe her, even if it happened to be true. People liked to think the worst.

"So what?" she said defiantly.

Elsie shrugged.

"Did he do it?"

"Do what?"

"Kill his wife when he saw the chance, after the place was done over."

"Of course not," said Felicity.

But was she really so sure? She couldn't believe that he would kill Emma because she, Felicity, had said she was going away. But what was the truth about his mother's death? What had that policeman been getting at? Norman had always been reluctant to talk about it. There was some mystery.

The atmosphere among her colleagues was strained, and the children stared at her with a frank interest which she found unnerving. One or two of the older ones called crude remarks after her as she crossed the playground, and at the end of the day the headmaster suggested it might be wise if she stayed away until things had died down. He would ask for a relief teacher, and perhaps she would consider making a permanent change. She was an excellent teacher, he added, and her private life was her own affair, but not when it impinged on the school.

Felicity was glad to be able to tell him that she had already applied for an overseas post.

Driving home, she suddenly remembered the conversation she had overheard in the pub before all this happened, when a group of youths had swaggered in and discussed what sounded like doing a break-in. She had completely forgotten it until now.

It couldn't have any connection. She struggled to remember what they'd said. Something about breaking a window and money not being kept in a till. She couldn't even remember what they'd looked like, except that they'd been full of energy, and one had worn built-up shoes which she'd noticed particularly. The publican might know them, though, if they were regulars.

She would have to tell the police, just so that they could be eliminated.

Mrs Costello had no reason now to get up in the morning. There was no snuffling damp nose thrust against her sleeping face; no one to open tins for or take for walks; no one to need her.

More terrible things happened than the death of a dog. Murder for instance, like Emma Widnes' death, and the business about that child. But these things had affected other people; Pedro's death was her own, and latest, tragedy.

A noise broke into her thoughts: the front-door bell. Kitty Minter, perhaps, come to nag her. She pulled the sheet over her head but the bell kept on. It might be the police. Now that it was too late, they were taking Pedro's death very seriously and had removed his blanket, which was covered in his hairs. She did not know why they were bothering. It was unlikely that they would seek Pedro's killer when they had a hunt on for someone who had murdered a woman.

The bell kept on ringing. She would have to get up.

She shuffled into her dressing-gown, shoved her thin, veined feet into her slippers, and padded downstairs.

Rose Hallam was at the door, her dachshunds beside her with their leads in a tangle.

"I've heard of a puppy that needs a home," she said without preamble. "It's a spaniel — a black one. It's to be put down if one can't be found by the end of the week. Will you come and see it?"

Mrs Costello shook her head.

"I don't want another dog," she said. "No one can take Pedro's place."

Rose, often rather timid, stepped forward until her foot was over the threshold.

"May I come in?" she said. "You'll get cold standing on the step." She couldn't let Mrs Costello stand there in disarray for everyone to see. "You get dressed while I make some coffee," she added. "Then we'll go together to look at the dog. Oh, isn't your garden lovely?" She moved to look at it through the window at the back of the hall. "Snowdrops and crocuses already — you'll soon have daffodils out. It's a very safe place for a puppy, isn't it? You could put a padlock on the gate at the bottom, so that mischievous boys can't undo it."

Mrs Costello did not take all this in straight away. She so mumbled, "I don't want another dog."

Rose smiled at her brightly.

"Go and get dressed," she said firmly. "There isn't much time."

"We've got him," Detective Inspector Cudlipp told Norman. "We can prove the break-in and the theft — he'd still got most of the money — and there were strands of his clothing on a bush in Mrs Costello's garden. But there's nothing to prove who assaulted Mrs Widnes."

Not yet: not unless forensic found something. Cudlipp spared Norman the final irony of hearing that there was now evidence of the robbery being planned in Felicity's hearing.

"You mean you still think I deliberately threw that safe on my wife's face as she lay helpless?" Norman said.

"As it happens, we don't," said Cudlipp. "But a clever lawyer, defending his client, could indicate such possibility."

"Doubts could be raised about the past, too," said Detective Superintendent Beddoes, in whose office this interview was taking place. "About your mother's death."

"I didn't kill her, any more than I killed Emma," said Norman. "Though God knows, I wished for her release."

Beddoes began doodling again on his blotter, adding to a fearsome pattern already there. At some point he must reveal that Emma had, in fact, died of a heart attack, but more might be learned from Norman first. The chance of getting any sort of confession out of Mick was slim. He was tough and amoral. But it could be proved that he had stolen the dog, and that he was the most likely person to have killed it. When forensic had finished with his clothing they might find dog hairs and bloodstains, human or canine, and the fact that the dog's head had been smashed, like Emma's, was a coincidence that could be emphasized.

"People may talk," Beddoes said. "Some have already. It could be very unpleasant."

Norman thought that nothing could be worse than it was now.

"Madge Pearce," he said. "What about her? She had no part in it, did she?"

"Against her will, yes," said the superintendent, for by now Madge had come round again and, when faced with the letter she had written, had broken down and disclosed what had happened between her and Mick. "He forced her to tell him where the safe was kept," Beddoes said.

"But what did he do?" asked Norman, and then, seeing the other men's faces, understood. "Oh — God, how awful! Will you charge him for that?"

"I doubt it. I don't think she'd be altogether willing, and he'd deny it — say she led him on," said Beddoes. "She may have, in a way, without realizing it. They went to a cinema and a pub together."

"Is she all right?"

"She'll get over the accident. As to the rest —" Beddoes smiled. "It's too soon to say."

"She must come back to the shop," Norman decided. "When she's well enough. If she wants to. She seemed happy with us —" he paused. "She seemed to like her job."

"It would be the best thing for her, I expect," said Cudlipp. Dr Barrett's prophecy was being fulfilled. Norman was preparing to adopt a new burden.

Beddoes had not finished. He drew a hatchet on the blotter before him. Then he asked:

"What happened when your mother died?"

Nothing would ever obliterate the details of that night from Norman's mind. He had entered the kitchen when Emma was mixing his mother's invalid food; she could tolerate little else now, and had grown quite fond of its bland texture, taking it sometimes with fruit flavouring or cocoa added.

On this occasion she had had a good day, even laughing at a programme on television before falling into one of her dozes, and had managed a thin slice of bread and butter for tea.

"You're putting a lot of sugar in it," Norman had said as Emma stirred the mixture, orange-flavoured tonight.

Emma had gone on stirring.

"It's how she likes it," she said, and had taken the drink to his mother. Norman had followed, and heard his mother remark on its bitterness; he had gone from the bedroom back to the kitchen and there, in a screwed-up paper bag in the wastebin, were a great many empty blue gelatine capsules.

When Emma left his mother's room, silently, he showed them to her.

"Ah yes. I was going to flush them down the toilet later," Emma said calmly. "You know it's for the best, dear, and you know you'd never be able to do it yourself. She's had a very good day. Let's hope she keeps them down."

She had taken the capsules from him and he'd heard the cistern flush.

Later, when she suggested they should marry, she said they both needed to feel safe. They were in it together; each was the other's accessory, and neither, in law, could then be made to testify against the other.

He knew in flat instant that her motive had not been mercy.

They had never mentioned the matter again.

"I've nothing to tell you," Norman said to Beddoes. "Nothing at all."

The publishers hope that this large print book has brought you pleasurable reading. Each title is designed to make the text as easy to read as possible.

For further information on backlist or forthcoming titles please write or telephone:

In the British Isles and its territories, customers should contact:

ISIS Publishing Ltd
7 Centremead
Osney Mead
Oxford OX2 0ES
England
Telephone: (01865) 250 333 Fax: (01865) 790 358

In Australia and New Zealand, customers should contact:

Bolinda Publishing Pty Ltd
17 Mohr Street
Tullamarine Victoria 3043
Australia
Telephone: (03) 9338 0666 Fax: (03) 9335 1903
Toll Free Telephone: 1800 335 364
Toll Free Fax: 1800 671 4111

In New Zealand:
Toll Free Telephone: 0800 44 5788
Toll Free Fax: 0800 44 5789

TELL THE WORLD
THIS BOOK WAS

Good	Bad	So-so

✓
✓ G

EB
Good MM.
CB
JC! Good

M S.

JW